Welcome to
Spirit Canyon, Texas

Nestled in the hill country, it's the kind of town where no one locks their doors, where neighbors stop and chat. At least that's what most people think. But there are secrets lurking in this tiny town. Secrets that harken back decades to unnatural events, unmentionable evil. And now that evil is about to be unleashed again.

In between potluck suppers and harvest festivals, people go missing. From behind ranch fences, livestock are found slaughtered, as if by an angry wolf. And in the cedar brush, strange chants echo in the moonlight. Is it the work of feral four-legged creatures, as they say, or fearless humans?

As the evil comes closer, centering on the good folk of Spirit Canyon, who will live to tell the tale? And who will believe it?

ELLE JAMES

BENEATH THE TEXAS MOON

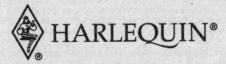

HARLEQUIN®

TORONTO • NEW YORK • LONDON
AMSTERDAM • PARIS • SYDNEY • HAMBURG
STOCKHOLM • ATHENS • TOKYO • MILAN • MADRID
PRAGUE • WARSAW • BUDAPEST • AUCKLAND

To my parents Charles and Phyllis Hughes
For always being there for me and showing me that hard work and perseverance pays off. Thanks for loving me unconditionally, teaching me to care about others, to laugh and play and to go after what I want with all my heart. Thanks, Dad, for being the rock in my life and a man I'll always look up to. Thanks, Mom, for being my sounding board and my best reviewer. You two helped to make me who I am. I'll love you always.

ISBN 0-373-88680-2

BENEATH THE TEXAS MOON

Copyright © 2006 by Mary Jernigan

www.eHarlequin.com

Printed in U.S.A.

ABOUT THE AUTHOR

2004 Golden Heart Winner for Best Paranormal Romance, Elle James started writing when her sister issued the Y2K challenge to write a romance novel. She managed a full-time job, raised three wonderful children and she and her husband even tried their hands at ranching exotic birds (ostriches, emus and rheas) in the Texas hill country. Ask her, and she'll tell you, what it's like to go toe-to-toe with an angry 350-pound bird! After leaving her successful career in information technology management, Elle is now pursuing her writing full-time. She loves building exciting stories about heroes, heroines, romance and passion. Elle loves to hear from fans. You can contact her at ellejames@earthlink.net or visit her Web site at www.ellejames.com.

CAST OF CHARACTERS

Eve Baxter—A woman who moves to Spirit Canyon in hope of getting her son's life back on track. Has she derailed into a terrifying nightmare?

Joey Baxter—The traumatized four-year-old who witnessed his father's mauling death by a vicious dog.

Mac McGuire—A battle-scarred ex-soldier determined to protect his home and the people he cares about.

Clinton Logan—Local attorney and mayor of Spirit Canyon. He rose fast in local politics. Is he too good to be true?

Toby Rice—Spirit Canyon's bully who's not above hitting a girl, but is he mean enough to kill?

Art Nantan—The man who loved Mac's mother and would have done anything to have her. How far did he go?

Addie Shultz—General store owner and grandmother Eve never had. Is there any truth to the stories she tells?

Daniel Goodman—Ranch foreman who took care of the ranch while Mac was away in the army.

Molly—Mac's Australian shepherd who protects those who can't protect themselves.

Prologue

Thirty years ago

"Thanks for bringing me home, Addie." Jenny reached to open the door to the pickup. "I'll see you tomorrow to finish the cleanup."

"You sure you don't want me to take you all the way up to the house?"

"No, thanks." Jenny patted her friend's hand and smiled, then she stared out at the night through the windshield of Addie's old truck. "George will be expecting you home soon. Besides, with the moon so full it's almost like daylight out here. And I could use a little fresh air after the festival."

Addie's face creased in a frown. "I'm gonna have a talk with Art. He had no right to be so rude to you. He knows you and Frank are crazy for each other. Even though he owns the notes on every piece of property in town, he doesn't have the right to be so rude."

Jenny sighed. "Don't worry about it. Go home. That's where I'm headed." She climbed down from the truck to stand in the caliche gravel and waved as Addie backed out onto the highway, easing her truck back toward town.

With a deep breath, Jenny inhaled the pungent scent of scrub cedar and dust. Although she enjoyed the clear, dry warmth of the night, she knew if it didn't rain soon, many of the ranchers would be devastated. Which would play right into Art Nantan's hands. He'd gone too far threatening her with foreclosure on her husband's ranch. But to threaten his Indian spirit magic was utterly ridiculous. Just because Art was of Apache descent, didn't make him any more intimidating in Jenny's mind. Nor did his magic talk scare her one iota.

As far as she was concerned, a man who threatened a woman wasn't much of a man. And why couldn't he understand that she was happy with her family? She was completely in love with Frank and her little boy, Mac. Her feet moved of their own accord, carrying her down the half-mile road to the house that had been part of her husband's family ranch for over a hundred years. Forward to her husband and son. Mac would be asleep already, but she still wanted to kiss him good-night.

After only a few steps Jenny sensed, more than heard, something in the scrub brush lining the gravel road. The hair on the back of her neck stood at attention and she strained her hearing to pick up even the slightest movement. Perhaps she'd been too quick to dismiss Addie's offer to drop her at her door.

Hadn't the ranchers been complaining about missing animals? Speculation had ranged from coyotes to wolves, and even the possibility of a mountain lion.

Her pace quickening, Jenny tried to shake off the uneasy feeling threatening to overwhelm her. She only had a half of a country mile between her and her family. She'd walked this road many times before in the moonlight.

As she rounded a bend on the gravel road, a dark shape leaped from the bushes, blocking her path.

Her heart clogging her throat, Jenny had to gulp in air before she could scream. Then she was running through the scrub cedar, the prickly branches tearing at her skin, slapping her in her face. But she ignored the pain. She had to get away. She'd never seen anything like this creature. And she knew beyond a doubt that if it caught her, she'd never see her family again.

Chapter One

Present

Black, billowing storm clouds churned the western sky, crowding in on the small town of Spirit Canyon. With a sigh, Eve Baxter parked her SUV next to the building with the words General Store etched into the stone facade across the top.

The surrounding shops and homes reassured her that, despite the threatening skies, this town was exactly what she'd hoped for. Clean sidewalks, white limestone structures and window boxes filled with purple and yellow pansies welcomed her. If the pansies were wilting and the paint fading on the store signs, she didn't care. At least she was away from the coastal storms of Houston and tucked securely in the Texas hill country. Spirit Canyon was a place Eve could feel safe—a place to call home.

When she opened her door and slid to the ground, a blast of wind whipped her hair into her face. She stretched her road-weary muscles and opened the rear door. "Come on, Joey. We're almost there. I just need to get the key from Miss Addie."

She wrapped a sweater around her son's thin shoulders and lifted him out of his booster seat. Once she'd set him on his feet, she tucked his hand in hers and gazed down into his face. She willed him to feel the hope, the chance to start over.

He held tight, his expression guarded—too intense for a four-year-old child.

"This is our new town, Joey. What do you think?" Eve smiled.

Joey crowded closer to her legs and didn't answer.

With effort, Eve forced herself to keep smiling. She'd give him time. Maybe in this new environment, Joey would snap out of his long silence and she herself could forget the dreams.

When she pushed open the rusty screen door, a bell jangled, the cheerful sound echoing through the building. Eve ushered Joey across the threshold into the store, standing for a moment to gain her bearings.

She inhaled the musty smell of ancient

timbers and the dust of a century. She felt as if she'd stepped into another time.

The hardwood floors were worn with age, and rows of shelves held everything from canned goods to bolts of cloth and fencing nails. Against the back wall stretched a long counter with an old cash register, three old bar stools and candy jars filled with jelly beans, gumdrops and licorice sticks.

She'd been right about Spirit Canyon. Her chest swelled with optimism.

"Don't just stand there, come on in." A white-haired woman, whose face was etched with a road map of wrinkles, counted change into the hands of a teenage girl. With a friendly flap of her hand, the older woman waved Eve and Joey toward the back where she stood.

A dark-haired, burly young man dressed in black, with silver chains draped from his pockets, stepped out from an aisle, grabbed the girl by the elbow and jerked her toward the door. "Let's go." He pushed past Eve and Joey, dragging the girl behind him, without a word of greeting or acknowledgment.

The girl smiled weakly and hurried to keep up.

Okay, so maybe her quaint new town had a dark side.

"I don't know what she sees in that boy. He's

always up to no good." The older woman's frown followed the pair out the door. Then she looked up and smiled at Eve.

"Addie Shultz?" Eve asked as she tugged Joey past rows of dry goods.

"Yes, ma'am. You must be Eve Baxter." The older woman looked at Joey and her gaze softened.

Eve cringed. She hoped Miss Addie wouldn't mention the jagged, red scar slashed across her son's face from his eyebrow up into his hairline.

Addie's short perusal shifted into a broad grin and she planted her fists on her narrow hips, staring down at the little boy. "And you must be Joey." She leaned over the counter and swept her hand in front of the treasure trove of sweets contained in old-fashioned jars. "Would you like some candy?"

Joey's eyes widened. He looked to Eve in mute appeal, his expression nervous but questioning.

Eve smiled and patted his hair. "Go ahead, baby."

"What will it be? Licorice, gumdrops, jelly beans…" Addie stopped listing candies when Joey pointed at the jellybean jar. "Good choice. Can't go wrong with a pocketful of jellybeans."

With a small metal scoop, she measured a generous portion of candy into a paper bag, twisted the top and handed it to Joey. "There you go, young man." She waved her hand to the left. "Why don't you sit by the game board while your mamma and I talk?"

Joey clutched his candy to his chest and shook his head violently, reaching up to grab Eve's hand.

"It's okay, sweetie. I'm not going anywhere without you." Eve led him to the table. "I'll be right over there. Sit and eat your candy while I talk with Miss Addie."

Eve stood next to Joey until he opened his bag and selected a bright red candy to pop into his mouth. While her son fished for another jelly bean, Eve slipped over to the counter.

"What a sweet little guy." Addie clucked her tongue. "Why does he look so sad and scared?"

Eve stared at her son, her thoughts on another day, not so long ago. The day the police had shown up on her doorstep. Even now the memory made goose bumps rise across her skin. Almost scarier than the police were the images she'd seen prior to the accident. The mauling had happened in her nightmares, and yet she had scoffed at them, thinking they were nothing more than aberrations.

"I'm sorry, it's none of my business." Addie ran a rag across the wooden counter.

With a shake of her head, Eve dragged her gaze back to Addie, her lips curving upward slightly. In a hushed voice she hoped Joey couldn't hear she said, "No, don't be sorry. The images are so vivid, sometimes I feel as if I'm still standing at my front door when they told me Joey and his father were at the hospital."

"Goodness." The hand pushing the old rag across the counter paused and Addie glanced up. "What happened?"

"A dog mauled them." Eve glanced back at her son's scarred forehead. "Joey only had superficial wounds and a few stitches."

Addie's eyes widened. "Dear God."

Her voice dropping even lower, Eve continued. "Joey saw his father mauled to death by the dog."

"You lost your husband? Bless your soul."

Eve shook her head. "My ex-husband. We'd been divorced for almost two years."

"Your decision or his?" Addie asked, then waved her hand. "That's too personal. Forgive an old lady's curiosity."

"No, that's okay. It was my decision." Eve shrugged. "He loved his dogs more than his family, and I had a son to raise."

The older woman picked at a button on the front of her shirt, her brow furrowed. "How long has it been since the mauling?"

Joey chewed quietly, his deep green gaze never leaving his mother's face.

"Six months." Eve smiled reassuringly at her son, although the strain of forced cheerfulness made her face hurt. Six months of pain. Six months of silence. Since the attack Joey hadn't spoken a word.

"The therapist said it'd take time." Eve turned her weak smile to Addie. "Speaking of which, I'll need to find a psychiatrist closer to Spirit Canyon."

"Should be some to choose from in Johnson City or Fredricksburg. If not, you could go to Austin or San Antonio." For several moments, Addie stared across at the little boy, tears welling, but not falling. Then shaking back her shoulders, she reached into her apron pocket and handed Eve two sets of keys. "I—" Addie cleared her throat and started over. "I went over earlier to open windows and air out the house. The place sure needs some work."

"I know." Eve swallowed past the lump blocking her vocal chords. She liked the way Addie had of getting back to business. The woman didn't wallow in the past. Thank goodness.

"What are your plans for that old house? Isn't it a bit large for just two people?" Addie sprayed furniture polish on the counter and rubbed a shine into the smooth wood.

"I was thinking of turning it into a bed and breakfast." Eve stared down at her purse. "I don't really need the money. My ex-husband left me as beneficiary to his life insurance policy. But I need the activity."

"You could work for me, just to keep you busy." Addie said.

Tears sprung into Eve's eyes. "You don't have to do that, Miss Addie. Besides, you hardly know me."

"Oh, fiddle." Addie waved her fingers. "We've talked so much on the phone, you're like one of my own younguns."

A lump rose in Eve's throat. Family was what she and Joey needed most. Eve twisted her purse strap. "I appreciate the offer, but I'll be busy fixing up the old place. If you know anyone who could help with the heavy stuff, let me know."

"Sure will." Addie slid the cloth further along the counter. "You know, our annual Harvest Festival is only a month away. If you get the bed and breakfast up and running by then, you shouldn't have any problem filling it."

Eve grimaced. "That's pretty close. I'm sure renovations will take longer than a month."

"I suppose that is a bit too soon." Addie

tapped a pencil to her chin. Then her eyebrows rose and she smiled. "Since you won't have the place opened by the Harvest Festival, how about helping with the preparations for the event?"

Eve hesitated. Being new to town, she'd hoped to ease into a quiet existence. "I don't know."

"I'm sure you'll have your hands full setting the old house in order," Addie continued, "but you'll have a chance to meet some of the townsfolk."

Eve hated to disappoint the woman when she'd done so much to welcome her. "You're sure I wouldn't be in the way?"

Addie waggled her fingers. "Not at all. And Joey is more than welcome. Other young mothers bring their little ones to the meetings. Joining the group will give Joey a chance to meet a few of the local children."

Eve glanced at Joey, his serious expression cutting through her reservations. He needed to learn how to be a child all over again. How better than to meet others his own age? Spirit Canyon was her new home, and she might as well get started by becoming a part of the community. "Addie, I'd love to help. Somehow I'll make the time."

"Good," Addie said. "I'll tell Sandy Johnson

and she can let you know when the next meeting will be."

The bell over the door jingled. Eve turned toward the sound.

A tall, broad-shouldered man stepped across the threshold. Poised in the doorway, with his face cast in shadows, he looked like the devil in a black Stetson.

"Mac? Is that you?" Addie called from beside Eve. "Better get inside before the heavens open up and dump on you, son."

"Yes, ma'am." His voice rumbled deep and resonant, filling the rafters of the store as he strode across the room.

Now that he'd moved into the light, Eve had to adjust her first impression. He wasn't the devil, especially when he smiled at Addie, with full lips, a rock-hard chin and eyes the pale blue-gray of a summer sky.

But the smile was short-lived. As he turned to face her, his penetrating gaze seemed to read her most intimate thoughts.

A chill stroked her spine.

He broke his eye contact and looked back out the screen door. "When did Cynthia start seeing Toby?"

"A couple weeks ago," Addie answered. "More's the shame."

The cowboy shook his head, turned and strode across the floor, closing the gap between himself and Eve.

She took a reflexive step backward.

"Mac, say hi to our new neighbor," Addie said.

He pulled his Stetson from his head, revealing dark brown hair with a hint of red, the rich color of molasses. He held out his hand. "Mac McGuire."

"Eve." Her voice faltered as she grasped his outstretched hand. Strong, work-roughened fingers engulfed hers, sending a startling jolt like an electrical current throughout her body. What was wrong with her? He was just a man.

Without his hat, he wasn't quite as intimidating. Until Eve saw the ragged scar slashed across his forehead.

Just like Joey's.

She dropped his hand.

Mac shifted his hat to his other hand. Besides the slight narrowing of his eyes, he didn't display any other indication that her reaction fazed him.

Eve stared around the room grasping for something to say, coming up with a blank. Then a gentle tug on her jacket changed her focus.

MAC GAZED DOWN at the little boy, whose fingers snuck into the hand of the auburn-haired woman. Eve. A woman with troubled green eyes.

With the same colored hair, the boy had to be hers. A sharp stab of disappointment raced through Mac until he noticed her naked left hand. She had a child, but no ring. Interesting.

The woman glanced down at the top of the little boy's head, brushed a hand through his hair and smiled. "Mr. McGuire, this is my son, Joey. Joey, say hello to Mr. McGuire."

Joey shook his head and buried his face against her legs.

Mac squatted next to Joey and spoke in a quiet tone. "Hi, Joey. Nice to meet you. You can call me Mac."

Joey peeked around his mother's leg and his eyes widened, his gaze zeroing in on Mac's scar. The boy moved toward him, instead of shrinking in fear. As one hand loosened its grip on Eve's jeans, he reached out to touch the mark on Mac's forehead.

Mac resisted the urge to flinch, holding steady while the little guy leaned toward him. When Joey's face cleared the fabric of Eve's jeans, it was Mac's turn to be startled. The child had a matching scar on the same side of his forehead.

A flash of memory assaulted Mac. Young men

under his command moving through the darkened streets of Fallujah. Mac closed his eyes, shutting out what had come next. When he opened them, Joey was staring at him as if he could see what Mac had seen. Mac frowned. What would a child know about the terrors of war?

While Joey ran his fingers over Mac's scar, Mac touched a finger to Joey's. "I see we have something in common."

He and the little boy had more scars in common than just the visible ones. By the serious look on Joey's face and the dark circles beneath his eyes, Mac knew the child had suffered.

With a grave but gentle nod to the boy, Mac straightened and looked at Joey's mother, noting the worry in her eyes. A long silence stretched between them. He sensed she was sizing him up while he did the same.

"Eve's looking for someone to help renovate the old Felton house." Addie sliced through the tension with her cheerful tone. "How about it, Mac? Could you spare time away from the ranch?"

Mac shifted the hat in his hand, staring at the broad brim. He had enough ghosts to chase without taking on more. What good would he be around this woman and her child who looked like they had their own problems to overcome?

With "no" poised on his lips, he looked up, his gaze meeting Eve's.

Her expression was wary and she hurried to say, "Oh, please, don't worry about it. I'm sure I'll find someone."

Although he'd been prepared to tell her he couldn't help, her quick rejection struck him in the gut. "Daniel and I could help her." Mac jammed his hat on his head. "He'd appreciate the break from ranch work."

"Great idea." Addie turned to Eve with a wink. "His foreman, Daniel, is so good with his hands. I swear he's renovated practically every house in the county at some time in the past forty years. He'd make a lot more money if he'd move to a bigger city. Not that I want him to leave. Just seems a waste."

"He claims he doesn't want to leave the ranch," Mac said. "And I couldn't function without him."

Addie sighed. "What's he gonna do when he runs out of houses to fix up around here?"

"Don't know. I guess he'll figure it out," Mac said. "Can I get some shotgun shells?"

Addie turned to a shelf behind the counter, calling over her shoulder, "What size?"

"30.06" he said.

"Ain't huntin' season." Addie placed the box

of shells on the counter. "Got varmints? Huckabee and Leider said they've been losing some of their young livestock lately. Think there might be a coyote or something pickin' 'em off. Funny thing is they ain't finding the carcasses."

"Yeah. I heard."

Eve's brows furrowed. "Should I be worried about…" She nodded toward Joey.

"Since we don't know what's doing it, I'd say it doesn't hurt to keep an eye on him." Mac stared down at the little boy who stared back at him, his look guarded.

"I will." Eve scooped Joey's hand into hers. "Well, I have a lot to do before bed tonight. I better get to it. Addie, I'll see you tomorrow." Eve waved and tugged Joey toward the door.

As the woman and the little boy walked away, Mac noted the view and couldn't help his instinctive tightening in reaction to a beautiful woman.

Before the door closed behind them, Addie cleared her throat. "Do you want these shells or not?"

"Huh?" Mac shook his head and dragged his gaze back to Addie. "Oh, yeah."

"She's a pretty little thing, isn't she?" Addie said, ringing up the purchase. "She and that little boy have been through some hard times."

When he handed her a twenty, he couldn't help asking, "What happened?"

Addie shook her head and sighed. "Little Joey and Eve's ex-husband were mauled by a dog. That little boy watched the dog kill his dad."

Mac turned back toward the door as if he could still see the little boy. He knew the pain of watching the people you cared about die. Worse, the guilt of being the only one who survived.

Mac shook his head and tried to imagine what Joey had gone through watching his father be killed by a dog.

Dog.

Mac dropped the shells on the counter and raced for the door.

"What's wrong, Mac?" Addie asked.

Just as he grabbed the handle of the door, an ear-splitting scream rent the air.

Too late.

Without slowing his pace, Mac flew through the door and toward the cries. After rounding the side of his pickup, he ground to a halt. His forty-pound Australian shepherd, Molly, lay on the ground with her chin touching the pavement, a worried expression on her wolfish face.

Standing between the dog and her SUV, Eve clutched Joey to her chest. The boy's body shook with the force of his screams.

Mac rounded the vehicles, scooped Molly into his arms, jerked open the door of his truck and deposited her onto the floorboard. He pointed a finger at her and ordered, "Stay!"

After shutting the door, he turned back to Eve and Joey, his heart hammering in his chest.

"It's okay, sweetie. The dog's gone. Mamma's got you. It's okay," Eve crooned, her voice wobbling. With her arms hugging Joey close, she backed away from the truck and hurried into the store, whispering words of assurance as she went.

Mac took a deep, steadying breath and ran a hand through his hair, then followed Eve. At the rear counter, he found Joey surrounded by the two women as if they shielded him from further attack.

Although Joey had stopped screaming, his eyes were red and puffy, and his body shook with silent hiccups and an occasional sob.

With a compelling need to make things right again, Mac removed his hat. "I'm sorry. I didn't know."

Eve looked over the top of Joey's head and smiled bleakly. "It's not your fault. There's nothing you could have done. He'd have seen a dog sooner or later. I had hoped it would be after we settled in."

"I'll keep Molly away from Joey in the future," he said.

"No, don't do that," Eve said. With her hand rubbing in steady strokes down her son's back, she stared into Mac's eyes. "He needs to get used to dogs. He can't avoid them forever." She rested her cheek against Joey's hair, a tear easing out of the corner of her eye.

The single tear slipping down to Eve's chin caused a meltdown in Mac's insides. For so long, he'd been plagued by self-recriminations, regret and sorrow.

Enough.

He straightened his shoulders, nodded and turned to leave. Maybe he could help Joey. And perhaps by helping the boy overcome his demons, Mac could shake a few of his own.

THE HOUSE WAS LARGE, the lighting dim, and it needed a heck of a lot of work, but it was hers. Eve pulled the sheet up to Joey's chin in the queen-size bed she'd share with him until his room was painted and ready. The air conditioner was on the fritz, and the night temperature was only a few degrees lower than the sweltering heat of the daytime.

Eve slid the window a little higher hoping to catch the breeze she'd enjoyed earlier that day.

But the overcast night air was still in the Texas hill country, shrouding the terrain in deep shadows. Shadows that could hide a coyote bent on preying on small animals.

Eve stared out the window. Her room faced out onto open scrubland and a nearby ridge, but the darkness was so dense, she couldn't make out anything past the light cast by the lamp in her bedroom.

When she pushed aside the sheet to lie down next to Joey, an eerie cry drifted in through the open window. Was it a coyote, a wolf or just a lonely dog?

Thank God, Joey didn't wake from his sleep. Even a dog's bark sent him into hysterics. Eve could imagine his reaction to howling in the night.

Inside her house, tucked safely behind sturdy walls, Eve couldn't stop the tremor that ran from the base of her skull down the length of her spine. The conversation she'd overheard between Addie and Mac McGuire about the missing animals resurfaced, settling like a knot in her belly. With a full day of work ahead, she lay still, willing her eyes to close and dreamless sleep to come.

Chapter Two

The rumble of an engine and the crunching sound of tires on gravel sent Eve to the front door. She shielded her eyes against the morning sun, staring up the driveway at the approaching charcoal gray pickup truck. Her heart sped up when she recognized it as the one Mac had driven the day before.

She touched her fingers to her hair then brushed away imaginary flecks of dust from her faded jeans and baggy T-shirt. Why was she getting all fidgety over the men scheduled to work on her house? Yet she couldn't stop the errant flutter of her heart as she stepped through the doorway to stand on the front porch.

Joey remained behind the screen door, peering out from the safety of the house.

"Aren't you coming out?" she asked. "It's Mac. The man from the store yesterday."

He shook his head, a frown denting his brow.

Eve sighed, but she didn't push him. The doctors had told her he'd come out of that shell on his own, given time and patience.

The truck stopped in front of the house, and Mac and another man climbed down. The two men were as different as storm clouds and sunshine—one dark and brooding, the other quite a few years older, but sunny and grinning.

With a deep, calming breath, Eve stepped from the porch and approached the men.

"Ms. Baxter…my foreman Daniel Goodman." Mac's voice contained as little expression as his unreadable face. "Daniel, Eve Baxter."

Eve held out her hand to the older man. With a leather tool belt draped around his hips, complete with tape measure, hammer and other tools hanging from loops, he looked the part of the capable handyman. His features were sundried, weathered lines boring into the corners of his eyes from squinting in the sun.

Daniel's hair had been dark perhaps in his youth, but now was heavily salted with gray, growing longish around his ears, as if he'd forgotten to get it cut. He smiled at her as he gripped her hand and pumped it. "Nice to meet you, Eve," he said. "I can't tell you how long I've wanted to get my hands on this house. Old lady Felton never wanted to change a thing."

"It looks like it." Eve laughed at Daniel's exuberance, caught up in his excitement. "I think the kitchen predates World War Two."

"I'm sure it does." Daniel glanced behind Eve. "And who do we have here?"

Eve turned and almost stepped on Joey. "Hi, sweetie," she said. "Come meet Daniel." She nudged him forward.

Daniel knelt to eye-level with Joey and stuck out his hand. "Nice to meet you, little buddy."

Joey stared from Daniel's hand to his face and back.

Eve held her breath, hoping he'd take the hand.

Her son had other plans. Joey turned to Mac, lifted both arms and stood on tiptoe.

Without missing a beat, Mac swung the child up in one arm. "Hey, big guy, what do you say you and I check out the yard while your mom and Daniel talk about the house?"

Joey nodded and hooked his arm around Mac's neck.

As Mac strode toward the gnarled live oak in the middle of the yard, Eve marveled at the contrast between Mac and Joey—one small and fragile, the other larger than life and powerful. For a child still displaying residual signs of the trauma he'd suffered, Joey had taken to Mac like a long lost friend. Eve wasn't sure how she felt about that. On the one hand, Joey's alliance with Mac could help bring him out of his long silence. On the other hand, Eve didn't want Mac hanging around.

He disturbed her.

"I see I have some work to do with Joey," Daniel said. "Mac sure has him won over, though. But that's Mac for you. He doesn't even try, and people are ready to lay down their lives for him."

"I'm amazed it's happened so fast." Despite her reservations, she knew a friendship with Mac could only be good for her son. "Joey could use a friend right now, and those two clicked from the start."

"Actually, Mac needs someone as well."

Daniel's words were spoken so softly, Eve thought she might have imagined them. Besides, Mac appeared very much in charge of his life. What benefit could he gain from a four-year-old?

The man in the black Stetson seated Joey on a low-hanging branch and pointed up into the leaves.

Eve thought this was how a father and son should look. She sighed at the futility of the idea. Mac wasn't Joey's father and never would be. The closest he could get was stepfather. And

Eve was determined to spare Joey from the same kind of pain she'd experienced while living under her stepfather's roof.

"How'd Joey get the scar on his forehead?" Daniel's question cut into Eve's thoughts.

She hesitated, her mind still mulling over the picture Mac and Joey presented.

Daniel hurried on. "You don't have to answer if it's too personal."

"No, I don't mind," she replied. "He was attacked by a dog. The same dog killed his father."

"Damn." Daniel shook his head. "Poor little guy."

Tearing her gaze from Mac and Joey, Eve asked, "How'd Mac get his scar?"

He tipped his head in Mac's direction. "Didn't he tell you?" He shook his head in answer to his own question. "Of course, he wouldn't."

"I just met Mac yesterday. We've barely said more than a few sentences to each other."

"Mac was in the Army up until three months ago." Daniel examined his boots then he glanced up into her eyes, his gaze seemed to look beyond her, beyond Texas.

"Was?" Eve sensed Daniel's reluctance to go on.

"Yeah." He stared at Mac's back. "He was so proud to serve his country. He was in the Special

Forces." Daniel inhaled deeply and blew out through his nose.

"What happened?" She touched a hand to his arm.

Daniel glanced at her, his eyes narrowing. Then, with an imperceptible nod he answered, "From what I could get out of him, his unit was ambushed while on a mission in Iraq. Mac took a bullet to his forehead and one in the leg."

Eve covered her mouth to hold back a gasp.

"The man's hardheaded. Only knocked him out." Daniel nodded in Mac's direction. "The leg wound meant he would never again go into battle. Next thing I know, he'd resigned his commission. Quit the Army." Digging his hands into his pockets, Daniel rocked back on his heels. "If you ask me, he hasn't been the same since. He works till he drops every day. I quit trying to keep up with him."

"How awful," Eve said. No wonder Joey and Mac were drawn to each other.

"Hey, don't say anything to Mac," Daniel said. "He'd kick me from here to tomorrow if he knew I'd told you."

"I won't say anything."

Daniel rubbed his hands together. "I came to renovate one very old and needy house. Where do you want to begin?"

Eve forced herself to concentrate on the task and led Daniel through the house. From one room to the next, she told him what she envisioned, and he gave her pointers and suggestions. When the tour was complete, they left through the front door.

Daniel marched the length of the weathered porch bouncing on the balls of his feet. "Some of these boards are warped and need to be replaced, and this column is practically rotted through. I'm surprised the roof isn't sagging. The good news is that the electricity was replaced fifteen years ago, the bad news is the exterior paint's peeling and the plumbing needs work. This renovation is going to cost."

"I expected as much. I've got the money set aside." Eve's gaze scanned the yard for her son. "Let me check on Joey."

"Great. I'll be just a minute," Daniel said.

While Daniel measured the boards, Eve ambled around the side of the house in search of Joey and Mac.

They squatted in a corner of the yard staring at the dirt.

Mac pointed down and talked in a low, steady tone, his words inaudible at that distance.

Joey listened, his eyes round and eager.

Mac reached over, pressed Joey's foot into

the dust and lifted it straight up. He pointed to the print Joey's shoe had made and to something in the dirt next to it.

Joey eyes lit with excitement at Eve's approach. He ran to her side, grabbed her hand and tugged her in Mac's direction. When they reached him, Joey poked a finger toward the powdery white dirt typical of the dry Texas hill country.

A perfect track of tiny shoe treads was set in the limestone dust.

"Is that your print, Joey?" Eve smiled at her son.

His head bobbed, and he pointed to the indentations next to his shoe print.

"What is it?" Eve asked.

"A deer track." Mac stood and brushed his hands along the sides of his jeans.

Eve's heart stirred. Mac had been showing Joey how to read tracks in the dirt. It was one of those man-things she would never have thought to teach her son. She frowned. This was the first time she'd considered how much Joey would miss by not having a father in his life. But a father was totally different from a stepfather. A father usually cared. Although, Joey's father had cared more for his dogs than his son. The odds were even worse with a stepfather. Hers hadn't cared, and he'd proven it over and over.

She straightened and looked up into Mac's eyes, immediately wishing she hadn't. This man had an effect on her, and she wasn't so sure she liked it.

"If you're through with my foreman, we have livestock to tend." His voice was low and resonant.

Assimilating his words, Eve looked up and repeated, "Livestock? What kind of livestock?"

"Cattle and goats. One of our breeder nannies disappeared some time over the past two days."

"I'm sorry to hear that," she said.

Mac shrugged and rubbed a hand over Joey's head. "See ya later, big guy. Bet if you look around, you'll find more tracks."

Joey hugged Mac around the kneecaps, and not two seconds later, he darted across the yard, stopping every two or three steps to check the ground.

Eve smiled at Mac. "I'm impressed."

A frown settled between his eyes. "About what?"

"I haven't seen Joey this carefree in months." Eve swallowed the lump in her throat. "Thanks."

"He's a great kid." Mac's gaze followed her son around the yard.

"I'm ready when you are." Daniel said as he sauntered over to the corner where Mac and

Eve stood. He smiled and nodded toward Eve. "I'll see you tomorrow, bright and early." The foreman climbed into the truck.

As Mac turned to follow, Joey raced up and grabbed his hand, tugging him back toward the house.

"I have to go now, Joey," Mac said. But he allowed the child to drag him a few more feet.

Joey pointed at a dry patch of dirt, and then looked up at the cowboy.

"Another track?" Mac squatted next to him. "Looks like a dog's print."

Joey's little body stiffened, and his glance darted from side to side as if he expected to see the dog. Then he spun and raced for the house.

Mac straightened and planted his hat on his head.

"Don't worry." Eve said. "He'll get over it."

Mac frowned down at the track. "Do you own a dog?"

"No," Eve answered. "Why?"

"This track is recent and fairly large."

"I heard an animal howl last night and it sounded pretty close." That eerie sound had echoed in her head until the wee hours. "Do you think it was the same one that left the print?"

"Most likely. You might want to keep an eye out for it."

"Do you think it could be dangerous?" A trickle of fear edged into her belly.

"Any strange animal could be dangerous. Wild animals usually don't stray close to town, but with you being on the edge, they don't always know the boundaries."

Mac nodded toward the house where Joey stood behind the porch rail, staring through the slats. "Just keep an eye out." He climbed in beside Daniel and the truck rumbled away.

Eve stared down at the dog track. Despite the heat of the Texas sun beating its late morning rays through the breaks in the clouds, goose bumps rose on her arms.

She shook back her concerns and took off for the house and the mountains of work awaiting her.

On the porch, she gathered Joey in her arms and hugged him close, inhaling his little-boy scent of dust and baby shampoo.

As she reached for the doorknob, the roar of an engine drew her attention back to the driveway, and she glanced up, half hoping Mac and his foreman had forgotten something. Instead of a truck, a shiny black Lexus pulled into the yard.

A man dressed in a gray suit stepped out of the car, brushing the fabric of his jacket smooth of wrinkles. Although of similar height and build to Mac McGuire, this man was strikingly handsome in a polished way, unlike Mac's rough exterior. His pale blue-gray eyes shown beneath sooty black brows and hair sprinkled with gray. Yet, despite the gray, he appeared to be about thirty.

He smiled, his grin engaging. He looked every bit the confident and successful business-man. "Ms. Baxter?"

"That's me." Eve returned his smile.

"Hi, I'm Clint Logan, mayor of Spirit Canyon." He held out his hand. "Welcome to our little town."

Eve shifted Joey onto one arm and reached out to shake the mayor's hand. "Nice to meet you."

Clint enveloped her hand in both of his and squeezed, holding on longer than necessary for a simple handshake.

Eve shrugged it off as the typical politician. When he finally let go, she rubbed her hand down the side of her jeans and stepped back, in-serting a little distance.

With his cheek pressed against her neck, Joey clutched the front of her shirt.

"As the mayor, I like to welcome new members of our community. I make it a habit to get to know all my constituents on a personal basis."

Eve's mouth quirked up on one side. "In a town the size of Spirit Canyon, that can't be too hard."

"True." Clint chuckled. "I hear you're helping with the Harvest Festival preparations. Did Addie strong-arm you into it?"

Defensive of her new friend, Eve hurried to reassure him, "No, no. I'm looking forward to helping. Addie said it would be an opportunity to meet some of the other people in the county."

"I'm sure a pretty lady like you won't have any problems meeting people. Folks love new-comers. Shoot, they welcomed me with open arms not five years ago, fresh out of law school."

"So, you're not a native of Spirit Canyon?" Eve asked.

"No, unfortunately. I'm from farther south, down by the border, outside Laredo."

"That's very impressive to be elected mayor after living here only five years."

"I think I got voted in because no one else wanted the job," he said with a wry grin.

Eve smiled. Clint was charming and good to look at. A very polished businessman. Quite a contrast to Mac McGuire.

"What are your plans, now that you're here?" he asked her. "Do you need a job?"

"No." She waved a hand toward the two-story

house with the sagging porch. "I'm hoping to turn the old house into a bed and breakfast."

"That's wonderful." Clint clapped his hands together. "The town could use a new bed and breakfast. Why don't we discuss your business plans over dinner? Perhaps I can give you some pointers, maybe even some legal advice on how to get started."

Eve hadn't expected a dinner invitation and she stammered a reply, "Thanks, b-but, I can't."

"Can't?" Clint's eyebrows rose.

Eve hurried to clarify her refusal. "I have so much to do to get the house in order so that I can open by Christmas."

"Surely you can spare some time to eat a bite?"

"Maybe another time." She wasn't sure she really meant it, but at least it bought her time to think about his offer. She could use the legal advice, but she'd rather not be in a one-on-one situation with a man.

Then why did her mind instantly recall that little intimate jolt of electricity she'd experienced the day before with Mac? She shook aside the memory and smiled at the mayor. "Thanks, anyway."

"If you decide differently, I'm in the office building two doors down from the General Store."

"I'll keep that in mind," she said aloud. And

avoid it, she added silently. Now was not the time to complicate her life.

Clint smiled again, climbed into his Lexus and rolled the window down. "Nice to meet you, Eve."

"Uh, Mayor Logan?" She walked toward his car.

"Ma'am?"

"Are wolves native to this part of Texas?"

His brows rose and he tipped his head to the side. "We don't get a whole lot of them this far south. We have been known to have coyotes around here, though. Why?"

"Just curious. What with all the problems the ranchers are having."

"I wouldn't worry about it. You're in town. Most animals won't come near a town. Now, if there's anything I can do for you, don't hesitate to ask."

"Thanks." Eve forced a smile and waved. Clint's answer to her question hadn't made her any less nervous. With Mac telling her to keep an eye out and Clint saying not to worry, she leaned toward the more cautious advice. That creepy howl still plagued her memory. She'd sure like to know what it was.

THE STEADY CLIP-CLOP of horses' hooves provided background noise in an otherwise still environment. Mac and Daniel had ridden over two hours, combing the four-hundred-acre ranch and finding nothing. They'd started by heading east away from town, dodging through brush, scrub cedar and live oaks. Molly had padded alongside Mac the entire way, keeping the pace set by the horses.

When the eastern side of the property hadn't turned up a goat or a rift in the fence, they headed west.

Each time the horses' hooves touched the ground, dust rose like a puff of smoke. A whirling gust of wind lifted the powdery soil and twisted it around the horse and rider, reminding Mac of another sandy day back in Iraq.

They'd been hunting the men responsible for the attacks on occupying American troops.

Mac inhaled deeply. The dust stung his lungs, but not like it had in Iraq. Too many times he had to inform himself he was in Texas. He was home. Thank God for Daniel. The only family Mac had left.

When he'd joined the Army, he'd found a family in his troops. Only to have them ripped away in an ambush. The same ambush in which he was hit in the leg and the forehead, knocked out cold and left to die. But fate had played a cruel trick. He'd woken up just as another convoy of American troops happened on the ambushed soldiers. As the soul survivor, he was destined to watch the cleanup of the dead young men—his men—who were little more than children themselves.

The medics had doped him up with painkillers and packed him off to a medical staging facility. They'd evacuated him from the country without giving him a choice. He'd wanted to stay and continue the fight.

At the Fort Bragg hospital, the doctors told him his knee was wrecked from the shrapnel. He'd never see battle again.

Several months had passed since he'd come home to the ranch, but Mac's memories were no less vivid.

Clouds hung low, pregnant with rain, yet holding back as if waiting for a signal from God to let loose. Mac was glad the rain held off. Two hours in the saddle was hard enough without the added aggravation of sliding in mud. He had a nervous feeling that had nothing to do with being on horseback for so long.

The feeling had a hell of a lot to do with one red-haired, green-eyed woman on the other side of the ridge in front of him.

His land bordered the edge of town. The last house on Main Street, Eve's house, was located next to the property line. He couldn't see it from where he rode, but he knew it was there. Eve and Joey were probably at home.

Mac and Daniel had ridden separately, but within shouting distance, for most of the search. As Mac neared the hill blocking his view of Spirit Canyon, Daniel joined him.

"Anything?" Daniel asked, reining in his horse beside Mac's.

"No." Mac scanned the countryside around them, searching the brown and green brush for the white goat.

The horses plodded along steadily, the tattoo of their hooves a soothing rhythm to Mac's heightened senses.

"It just doesn't add up." He stared out across the brush land.

"What?"

"Leider lost a couple lambs less than a week ago. Huckabee's missing a two-month-old Hereford calf. You'd think they'd at least find the carcasses."

"Yeah. Kinda hard to lose an entire calf without finding a carcass." Dan removed his straw hat and combed his fingers through his hair. "At least with a body, you have half a chance of figuring out what ate it. Hard to protect your livestock when you don't know what's stalking them."

"We lose the young all the time. But we're looking for a full-grown goat. You'd think we'd have found her by now."

"Don't look now, but I think we have." Daniel nodded ahead.

Molly bounded to a spot a few hundred yards in front of them, barking wildly, scattering a half-dozen buzzards clustered on the ground. She sniffed the pile of skin and bones, and then tipped her nose skyward and howled, a long, eerie sound, shattering the stillness of the day.

The clumsy birds flapped their wings, heaving themselves from the ground into the air. Once aloft, they rose gracefully to circle and wait for the humans to move on.

With a sharp tug on his reins, Mac stopped his horse several feet from the picked-over carcass and swung to the ground. The smell of blood and dust assailed his senses, rendering useless his ability to block the memories of other bloody bodies strewn in the sandy streets of Fallujah. Mac's gut clenched and churned, lifting the bile to his throat.

"What a waste." Daniel's words cut through Mac's thoughts. "She was a good producer."

With the toe of his boot, Mac nudged at something in the dirt. It was a yellow plastic ear tag with the number twenty-one on it. Mac studied the rocky ground around the goat, but the birds had disturbed any loose dirt. He couldn't discern animal prints in the dust.

"What do you suppose got her?" Daniel asked.

Mac shook his head and widened his search in a growing circle. Nothing. Not a footprint, pawprint, disturbed grass or droppings from anything other than the greedy birds and Molly.

"I heard Mr. Largey say they'd seen a cougar around these parts last year," Daniel said as he scanned the surrounding hills. "I hadn't heard any more about it this year. I know they can have a pretty wide range."

"You think a cougar did this?" Mac asked.

"Who knows? Could be anything. Been a rumor about some kind of cult in the county sacrificing animals and all. Suppose they got hold of her?"

"No." Mac shook his head. "An animal did this." Maybe a cougar. His gut clenched. Or maybe a dog. A big dog.

With her nose to the ground, Molly trotted away from the carcass.

Mac followed the dog until they reached the crest of the hill overlooking the little town. Molly paused and stared down the steep incline. Then she looked back at him and whined.

Spirit Canyon sprawled quietly in the meager,

late-afternoon light, a few cars ambling along Main Street toward the Community Center. Addie had mentioned something about today being the annual Harvest Festival planning committee meeting. Should be a lot of people crowded into the Community Center. Mac could see Eve's house, the old tire swing hanging from a tree in the backyard.

"Damn." Mac frowned.

"Did you find anything?" Daniel joined Mac and followed his gaze. "Damn."

"No kidding."

Daniel shook his head. "Awful close to town."

"Yeah."

"You don't suppose whatever animal did this would attack during the daylight?"

"Most predatory animals are nocturnal," Mac said. But he knew animals with rabies would attack day or night.

A movement caught his eye. Eve and Joey left the house and were walking down the street toward the Community Center.

"Whatever it was took out a pretty big goat. Almost as big as a man," Daniel said.

Definitely larger than a child Joey's size.

Mac looped the reins over the saddle horn and swung up into the seat. "Better warn the neighbors."

Chapter Three

Exhausted from a full day of scrubbing floors and windows, Eve hung up her cleaning rag. With Joey in tow, she left the house and walked to the Community Center, only four blocks away.

With her head tilted toward the troubled sky, Eve ignored the oppressive cloud cover and let the ambiance of the small Texas town wash over her. What a wonderful feeling to be in a place where she could walk anywhere she wanted or needed to go. To belong to a community where she could get to know everyone on a first-name basis. How different from Houston where she didn't even know her next-door neighbor.

Yet, after the discovery of animal prints in her front yard, she wasn't foolhardy enough to go without some protection. She tapped the end of the long walking stick on the ground with each right footstep. If something were to attack her, she'd come out swinging with enough ferocity to scare it back into the hills.

Halfway to the Community Center, she passed a five-foot-tall wooden fence. Behind it, an animal sniffed the base as they walked by. A gap at her level revealed a large black and tan rottweiler. Eve didn't make a big deal about it, afraid Joey would freak out if he suspected a dog lurked behind the wooden slats.

Still, she couldn't help wondering if this dog had left the pawprints in her yard, assuming the owners let him loose. She'd ask Addie.

Before reaching the door to the concrete block building painted the color of white limestone, she could hear the hum of voices from within. Excitement and nerves tweaked her stomach.

Joey dropped her hand and hooked his arm around her knee.

With a pat to her son's head and a deep breath, Eve pushed through the screen door and stepped into the crowded building. She scanned the room for a familiar face and was about to give up when she spotted Addie.

The older woman smiled and waved. "Howdy, neighbor!" Addie weaved through the men and women to reach Eve's side. "Glad you decided to join us."

"I'm not so sure this was a good idea." Eve tipped her head toward Joey.

"Give it a chance." Addie patted her arm and drew her farther into the large room.

Walking was difficult with Joey clinging to her leg, but she managed to maneuver to the back of the building near a large serving counter. Men and women stood or sat in the available chairs, smiling and chatting in the way old friends do.

Like an outsider looking in, Eve wondered if she'd ever be this comfortable with the locals. She hadn't grown up here, why should they accept her? Her mother and stepfather had moved every three or four years while Eve was growing up. She'd never felt like she belonged anywhere.

The same young man she'd seen yesterday in the General Store sat on the counter with the same teenage girl trapped between his knees. Today, he wore a muscle shirt exposing his broad shoulders. Tattooed on one was the face of a fanged wolf.

Eve fought a shiver. The guy was just creepy.

Without slowing her pace, Addie said, "Get off the counter, Toby Rice."

Toby sneered. "You gonna make me?"

She tucked in her chin and glared up at him with a "don't mess with me" look. Then her attention turned to the teenage girl. "Your daddy know who you're hangin' out with, Cynthia?"

"Yes, ma'am." Cynthia smiled back at her.

Eve was surprised at the contrast between the insolent bulk of a young man and the slip of a sandy blond-haired girl who couldn't be more than sixteen.

"Man ought to have his head examined." Addie planted a fist on her hip and stared up at Toby. "You gettin' off that counter or am I gonna have to have the sheriff remove you?"

"Ooo. I'm so scared." Toby shot her a narrow-eyed look, his voice dripping sarcasm.

"Good thing your mother ain't alive to see how rude her boy turned out." Addie shook her head. "That woman was a saint. She didn't deserve the likes of a bad-tempered, bad-mouthed, snot-nosed punk like you."

Toby shoved Cynthia away and hopped off the counter to stand toe to toe with Addie Schultz. "Don't you say nothing about my mother, you hear me?"

To her credit, Addie showed no fear, even though the big guy could have snapped her neck with one hand. "Grow up, Toby."

"You'll regret messin' with me," Toby rumbled in a low, menacing voice.

Cynthia stood to the side, her forehead

creased in a frown, her hands clenched together. Toby grabbed her arm and jerked her toward the door. "Come on. This place sucks."

"But I wanted to see Aunt Lois," Cynthia said, her voice sounding soft and slightly apologetic.

"Forget it. We've got plans." Toby jerked her arm again.

Cynthia leaned away. "I don't want to go. Why don't you go without me?" She twisted her arm, trying to loosen his hold.

"No way. You're expected to be there with me. You're going." His hand squeezed tighter until Cynthia winced.

Tired of Toby's bullying, Eve stepped forward. "She said she didn't want to go with you. Perhaps you should let go of her arm, Mr. Rice."

The young man towered over Eve and snarled. "Who are you, anyway? And who made you the law?"

She refused to be intimidated. "Eve Baxter, and no one made me the law. But you should treat her with respect, not like some piece of meat to jerk around."

"She's my girl. I treat her any way I want."

Addie crossed her arms over her bosom. "Not if she don't want it and not with me around."

"Don't piss me off." Toby warned, his eyes tapering to a squint.

Eve and Addie stood their ground, refusing to back down.

Toby glanced from one woman to the other, and then snorted, turning toward the door. "Had enough of this place." When he passed Cynthia, he shot over his shoulder, "You comin' or not?"

Cynthia frowned at Toby's back and then shrugged at Eve and Addie, her gaze cast down. "I'm coming." Before another word was spoken, the two disappeared out the door.

Addie clucked her tongue. "I don't know what a sweet girl sees in that good-fer-nothin'. I've a good mind to talk to her daddy." Then she shook her head. "Never mind him."

She took Eve's hand and led her over to a couple closer to Eve's age. At their feet, a girl about the same size as Joey played with a plastic bag full of rocks.

"Tom, Laura and Katie Taylor, this is Eve and Joey Baxter. They just moved to Spirit Canyon." Addie turned to Eve. "Tom and Laura moved from Amarillo last January."

The little girl shoved chubby hands toward Joey. "See my fossil?" In her palms was a chalky white rock the size of Eve's fist.

Joey stared at the rock and then up at Eve.

Eve held her breath, hope rising like adrenaline in her system. She prayed Joey wouldn't shy away from this attempt at friendship.

"Don't you like fossils?" Katie tipped her curly blond head to the side.

Joey nodded but didn't let go of Eve's leg. At least he hadn't hidden behind her.

"Here, you can have this one," Katie said. When Joey still didn't move, she set the rock on the floor and dug in her bag for another.

The boy sat on the floor and reached for the rock and held it in his hands.

"I got 'nother one. See?" Katie held out her hand.

This time, Joey took the rock.

Katie stared up at the scar on Joey's face. "You got a booboo." She went to Joey and pressed a kiss to his forehead. "I kiss it better."

Joey didn't shrink back. He scooted closer to Katie's bag of rocks.

Eve straightened and smiled at Tom and Laura. "Nice to meet you," she said, and meant it. Addie was right, Joey needed other children to remind him how to act like the child he was.

"It's hard moving to a new place and starting over. I imagine it's even harder when you're a single parent." Laura squeezed her husband's hand.

Tom laughed. "I'm beginning to wonder if

we picked the wrong year to come. What with the drought, we'll be lucky if we can pay back our loans at the end of growing season."

When a familiar voice spoke in a low, rumbling tone to a group of folks behind Eve, every hair on the back of her neck rose in salute. Without looking in that direction, she could sense Mac had entered the Community Center. She couldn't resist easing her head around, just enough to see him through the corner of her eye.

Just like the day before, Mac stood with his hat shading his face from the overhead lights. He moved through the crowd, stopping to shake hands with fellow ranchers.

Heart rate speeding up, Eve turned to Addie, hoping her face would cool by the time Mac reached the back of the store.

"So, Eve, are you up for a little meddling from all your new neighbors?" Addie winked at Eve. "Most folks around here see a single female as a challenge."

Eve shook the man out of her head and concentrated on what Addie was saying. "What kind of challenge?"

"We're still in the old-fashioned mind-set. A woman can't possibly be happy unless she's married."

Eve's stomach knotted. "Been there, done that, got the scars and the divorce decree to prove it."

"I'm sorry to hear that. It must have been hard." Laura leaned into her husband. "Not every marriage ends in divorce, though. Right, sweetie?"

Tom squinted, a smile toying with the corner of his mouth. "Is this the place where I'm supposed to answer 'Yes, dear'?"

Laura dug an elbow into his ribs, but Tom pulled her close for a loud, smacking kiss.

Eve smiled. She wished she'd had such a relationship with her husband. But he'd been more interested in himself and his dogs than her and Joey.

"I take it you're not on the market?" Laura asked Eve. "Officially or unofficially?"

Eve blushed. "Unofficially. I'm not interested in dating right now."

"What a shame. And I'd hoped to convince you otherwise." Warm hands gripped her shoulders to turn her around.

Eve stared up into Clint Logan's blue-gray eyes. "Like I said, I'm not interested."

"I can be very persuasive. Am I right?" He winked at Addie.

Eve shook her head. "I have Joey to consider."

"And why would your dating be a problem for Joey?" Clint asked.

"I'm not in the marriage market and I won't force a stepfather on Joey," she said.

Addie tipped her head to the side. "Don't you think a boy needs a man in his life?"

Years of heartache surfaced, blocking Eve's throat. All the times she'd tried to do just as her stepfather wanted in order to gain his respect and love. As she had in the past, she swallowed her disappointment. "Not always. Depends on the man."

Joey jumped up from the floor and raced past Eve.

"Hi, Joey, whatcha' got?" Deep tones rumbled immediately behind her.

Tingly surges raced across her nerve endings. That voice could only belong to Mac.

Eve turned as Joey launched himself into Mac's arms and waved his rock beneath the cowboy's nose. The two looked as though they belonged together, like father and son. How she wished Joey could have had a father like Mac. But Mac could never be his father; the best he could be was a stepfather. And Eve wasn't going there.

"I don't see anything wrong with a son being raised by his mother." Clint stepped closer to Eve and laid a hand on her shoulder. "A mother loves and protects her children. She stands by them and defends them no matter what."

Mac's head jerked up at the words. His jaw tightened and his brows dipped slightly.

"Did I say something wrong?" Clint shrugged his shoulders.

But Mac only stared hard into Clint's eyes and then broke the visual contact to look down at Joey. "I like your rock, Joey. Keep your eyes open, and you'll find lots of sea fossils in the hill country." Mac set the child on his feet, tipped his hat at Addie and strode over to a group of men.

Addie shook her head at Clint. "Wish you hadn't said that to Mac."

"Am I missing something?" The mayor gazed after Mac, an apologetic frown creasing his brows.

"No. You're not missing anything. Why don't you go do your politicking with the ranchers?" Addie pushed Clint away from the little group. "Go on, shoo!"

"Okay," he said, moving away. He glanced back at Eve and smiled. "But I still want to take you to dinner, Eve."

"Thanks for the offer, but I'm—"

"I know. Not interested." Clint nodded. "I'm patient, I can wait."

MAC HALF LISTENED to the local ranchers and businessmen discussing plans for the Harvest Festival.

He'd never been one to join in the planning, choosing to help out when the time came to build booths and make repairs to the community building where the dance would be held.

Out of the corner of his eye, he watched Eve smiling and talking with Tom and Laura. Her laughter floated to him, hitting him in the gut. Mac turned away before he started thinking of something as ridiculous as white picket fences and a yard filled with children remarkably similar to Joey.

When talk about the festival tapered off, Mac brought up the topic he'd come here to discuss in the first place. "I found one of our breeder goats just over the hill from town." Everyone within hearing distance turned toward him. "Wasn't much left for the buzzards."

"That's too bad, Mac." Bernie Odom looked up from playing checkers with Hank Bleumfeld. "Have anything to do with the drought?" he asked.

"No." Mac glanced down at his hat and back up to Bernie. "Looked like an animal attack."

"Any idea what?" Sheriff Hodges twirled an unlit cigarette in his fingers but didn't light up. He'd told Mac he was in the second week of his campaign to quit smoking after thirty years in the habit. "We've had several reports come in about missing animals in the area. Might be a pattern."

Mac shook his head. "Too dry for tracks. But whatever it was had to be big enough to take down a goat weighing more than a hundred pounds."

"I'm missing a lamb, haven't seen her since the day before yesterday," Tom said. "Thought maybe its mother wasn't feeding and left it laying somewhere out in the brush. I looked, but didn't find a carcass. Not even any buzzards."

"I lost a calf last week," Bernie Odom said. "I found it, but the buzzards had taken care of the remains. Didn't think much of it at the time. You tend to lose the small ones for one reason or another. Especially as dry as it is out here. But a breeder is an entirely different story."

"Kinda reminds me of way back when we had the big drought some thirty years ago. Animals kept disappearing all mysterious like," Bernie mused. "Think it ended up being a wolf. Isn't that right, Hank?"

Hank's hand hesitated over a game piece, and he glanced over at Art Nantan, the feed-store owner. "That's right. Got quite a few lambs, goats and a couple calves."

"Took one of my prize Merino lambs that year

my breeder came in first at the state fair," Art said and shrugged. "Happens when you're in ranching. Thank God I'm not ranching anymore."

"Nor are a lot of us," Jack Adams grumbled. "If it weren't for droughts and the animals dying, the big farming and ranching conglomerates were going to put us out of business eventually. Sure miss the old place, though."

"What are you complaining about?" Art asked. "You telling me you don't want to work at the feed store?"

"No, no," Jack said. "You know I appreciate havin' the work. I just hated losing land that had been in my family for a century."

"Probably better off. Those of us who've managed to hold out are barely makin' ends meet." Hank scratched his head and shrugged. "The drought ain't helpin', and if there's something out there pickin' off the livestock, won't be a lot to show at the market next year."

"Yeah. Guess I'll have to bring in the lambs and goat kids at night," Tom said.

"You gonna bring in the breeders, too?" Bernie pulled a round can from his back pocket, pinched a wad of tobacco and shoved it just inside his mouth between his bottom teeth and gums. When he'd pushed it into place, he spoke over the lump behind his lip. "Can't figure.

Haven't seen wolves in these parts since that last time. Maybe it's just a coyote."

"Maybe. Wolves don't normally come this far south." Hank studied the game board. "You gonna play or flap your gums?"

Ignoring his partner, Bernie nodded toward Mac. "That last time was bad because Jenny McGuire was attacked by the critter. That's how come we know'd it was a wolf."

Mac's stomach tightened. He didn't want to hear the story he'd heard all his life. It always ended the same.

"She'd been Homecoming Queen the year she graduated high school. I remember. I was captain of the football team, so I got to escort her down the aisle at the coronation." Sheriff Hodges stared at a corner of the room as if seeing into the past. "She was the most beautiful girl in the county, with all that long, black hair and those blue eyes. A guy could see all the way to China in 'em."

"She was a pretty little thang, until that wolf got hold of her," Bernie said, concentrating on the checkers.

Mac almost turned to leave when he noticed that Eve, Laura and Addie had joined the group.

"She never was the same after that." Bernie chewed on his tobacco. "Left town a few months later. Mac was too young to remember most of it. Ain't that right, Mac?"

Not young enough to forget, Mac thought. His mother had left her husband behind to pick up the pieces. Mac's only response to Bernie's question was tightened lips. The pain and anger had long since evolved into a dull ache that never seemed to go away. Even after thirty years. "Point is," Mac said, interrupting Bernie's story, "whatever got that goat did it over the past two days, not thirty years ago."

"Think whatever done it might still be out there?" Addie asked.

"Yes, ma'am." Mac inhaled deeply and let it out. He hadn't realized how tense he'd gotten. "Although predators come out mostly at night, it doesn't hurt to keep an eye on the little ones." His glance rested on Joey and Katie where they sat on the floor just beyond the group of adults, sifting through the collection of fossils. Here in the Community Center they could play happily, oblivious to the danger that lurked near town. Outside the limestone block walls, who knew?

Eve's voice pulled him back. "You don't think Joey's in danger from whatever killed the goat, do you?" Her words wobbled and her face paled.

"It doesn't hurt to be overly cautious. Keep

an eye on him and don't let him wander far from the house."

"Speak of the little devil, looks like someone's getting tired." Addie nodded toward Joey.

He set the rock he'd been holding on the ground and stood, rubbing bunched fists into his eyes.

"Come on, Joey, we should go." Eve smiled at Tom and Laura. "It was really nice meeting you. Let me know what I can do to help with the Harvest Festival."

Mac found himself envious of that smile. Would she ever turn to him with such a smile? Did he really want her to? She'd pretty well stated her stance on relationships. She wasn't interested in another man in her life. Not that he was the one for her. His mother had left him and he'd watched as his father died of a broken heart. Not to mention, Mac had failed his men in combat. How could he possibly add any value to Eve's life?

Joey walked out the door ahead of Eve.

"Joey, wait a minute." Mac moved to snatch Joey up in his arms.

Mac's chestnut horse stood next to the curb tied to a lamppost. Molly lay on the ground next to the big beast, her stumpy tail flicking side to side.

Eve eased up beside Mac, a questioning expression on her face until she spied the horse and dog.

Joey buried his face in Mac's black T-shirt, his hands clutching the fabric, turning his knuckles white.

"It's okay, Joey," Mac said in a low, steady tone, coaxing the little boy to look up. "Molly won't hurt you. Watch how her backside wiggles when she's excited. That means she likes you."

Joey peeked through one eye at the dog. The Australian shepherd wagged her stump and spun around in a circle.

"Molly's special," Mac continued, his voice smooth and calming. "She takes care of our little animals. She's like a babysitter. When a baby goat or lamb loses its mother, Molly takes care of them. And she's different than most dogs. If you look close, she has one blue eye and one brown."

Turning his face more so he could see the animal with both eyes, Joey stared down at the dog dancing in the light from the lamppost.

While Mac held Joey, Eve stepped closer. He could smell her subtle fragrance between the few inches separating them. When his body tightened in response to her nearness, he shifted away.

Molly stopped dancing and sat, her ears perked, tongue lolling. The animal's long coat was a mix of black, brown, silver and white smeared and spotted in a unique pattern.

The odd-colored eyes made some people think she was strange and maybe dangerous. But Mac knew there wasn't a vicious bone in the dog's body. "She may look mean, but she'd give her life for her family."

Eve looked up into his eyes. "And family's important to you, isn't it?"

Her words shot straight to his gut, re-opening old wounds, exposing him to her intense stare. Caring for someone had only left him vulnerable. Before he could think too much about his mother, his father and the troops he'd let down, he raised the shield around his heart. "You better get him home. He's all done in."

Even with the dog standing in front of him, Joey was falling asleep in Mac's arms. His body felt warm and soft. Soft was something Mac couldn't afford to feel or be.

Without another word, he handed Joey to Eve. "If you'll wait just a minute, I'll walk you home."

"No need," she said a little too quickly. "I'll be fine. It's only a few blocks."

Apparently, he made her as uncomfortable as she made him. But the thought of her walking alone with some killer animal that close to town made his skin crawl. "Wait here. I'm going to walk you home. But first, I need to make sure Daniel follows me with my mount so I'll have a way to get back to the ranch." He tipped his hat and ducked back into the building. He'd walk her home despite his internal warning bells telling him to stay clear of this woman.

EVE DIDN'T WAIT for Mac to return. She could be halfway to her house by the time he rejoined her. Before she'd gone a block, Joey was fast asleep on her shoulder, deadweight in her arms. The rain remained only a promise, for which she was temporarily thankful. But the cloudy skies kept any hint of moonlight from illuminating her path. And, as she was learning was typical of small towns, streetlights were nonexistent.

With care for uneven sidewalks and pavement, she made her way toward her house at the end of Main Street.

When she passed the fence with the rottweiler, the dog followed them along the fence line, sniffing like he had before. Almost at the end of the row of slats, the dog snarled menacingly. Eve held her hand over Joey's ear to keep him from waking to the sound. When she'd cleared the fence and hurried on, the dog slammed against the boards. His maniacal barking stirred Joey from his sleep.

"It's okay, Joey, go back to sleep," she said, picking up the pace to increase the distance between her and the crazed dog.

Then the rottweiler squealed like a scared pup, and quiet resumed.

Eve breathed a sigh of relief, wondering why the dog shut up, but more interested in getting Joey home than finding out.

Two blocks away from the house, she heard a twig snap. She'd been walking on the street to avoid the ups and downs of the sidewalk in the dark. And the street was clear of all sticks and leaves. A shiver shook her body from the base of her neck to the small of her back. Had the dog gotten loose?

Eve spun around, fully expecting to come face-to-face with an angry canine. In the little bit of light from the windows of nearby houses, she could see nothing. No dog, no bogeyman, only deep, menacing shadows. She really needed to get a grip on her overactive imagination.

The story about Mac's mother must have shaken her more than she cared to admit. That, coupled with Mac's warning to watch out for Joey, gave her the creeps. He'd said the animal stalking the community's livestock might be nocturnal. Surely it wouldn't venture into human territory, like right here on Main Street.

She lengthened her stride, just short of a jog. Home never seemed so far.

Another twig snapped and leaves crunched behind her.

Eve stopped dead in her tracks. If there was a wolf or coyote out there, she still had to get to her house. Should she go back to the center and wait for Mac or continue on? If she went back, she'd have to pass in front of the rottweiler. Was the animal still behind the fence? She stomped her foot when she realized she'd left her walking stick back at the Community Center. Not that she could have held it and a sleeping Joey at the same time.

Where Eve stood, the houses lining the street were dark. With no moon and no other lights available, Eve hesitated in the gloom debating her next move.

A low rumbling stirred the air. Too near for thunder and too much like a growl.

Straining her eyes, Eve stared into the shadows, clutching her son tighter. Nothing. No movement, no eyes staring back. Then the rumbling sounded again, deeper and more drawn out.

The second repetition was enough. Eve spun on her heel to race back to the Community Center. But she hadn't gone two steps when she plowed into a brick wall with sufficient force to jolt Joey awake. Eve sucked in enough breath to fill her lungs twice and opened her mouth to scream.

Chapter Four

Mac staggered back a step to absorb the full impact of Eve, armed with Joey, barreling into his chest. He grabbed Eve's shoulders to steady her as she stumbled backward.

Her mouth opened, but she looked up into his face and the scream died before it was born. "Oh, thank God." She collapsed against him.

Squashed between the two adults, Joey whimpered and glanced around, blinking. When he spied Mac, he reached out.

Mac tucked him against his side, holding on with one arm. The other wrapped around Eve's shoulders and pulled her close.

Beneath his fingers, he could feel tremors shaking her body. He pressed her face to his shoulder, stroking her hair. "It's okay. Shh. I've got you now. Everything will be okay."

She didn't pull away, but rested her cheek against his chest, clutching the fabric of his shirt.

Almost as shaky as Eve, Mac willed his heart to slow to a normal pace. When he'd exited the Community Center and she hadn't been there, he'd had the closest thing to a panic attack he'd ever admit to. The same gut instinct that told him he and his men were walking into a trap hit him with enough force to knock him back a few steps before he could get his feet moving in the right direction. He couldn't be too late this time. He couldn't let Eve and Joey down like he had his troops.

When she'd walked right into his arms, all he could do was press his face against her soft hair, inhaling the scent of herbal shampoo. She smelled like spring, a sharp contrast to the dry, sandy heat of Fallujah. Thank God she was all right.

As soon as his heart returned to normal, his protective instinct warred with past experience. What right did he have to hold this woman and promise her things would be fine? Though he'd found her unscathed, hadn't he proven he couldn't take care of those he loved?

Without opening his eyes, Joey nestled his face into Mac's neck and fell asleep, his head tucked beneath Mac's chin.

Eventually Eve stopped shaking and rested in the circle of his arm. She lifted her face and smiled, her bottom lip trembling. "I'm sorry. It's just…" She stared down at her fingers knotted in his shirt. A moment later she released her grip and stepped back. "The stories, your warning…I don't know. I started hearing things and the next thing you know, I'm running back the way I came."

"I'm glad you did." Mac reached out and brushed a lock of hair from her cheek. Her skin was as soft and smooth as he'd suspected, and he wanted to trail his hand down her jawline to touch the pulse hammering in her throat. His hand dropped. "Why didn't you wait for me?"

"I didn't want to trouble you." She looked down at her shoes. "I wanted to go alone."

"And now?" His finger hooked under her chin and tilted up her face. He cursed the lack of street lamps, wishing he could read her expression.

"I'm glad you're here." Eve backed up another step until Mac's arm dropped to his side. "I don't know what came over me. I'm not usually such a wimp, but being in a strange place, I'm not used to the sounds."

Mac stared around at the shadows, the hairs on his arms rising. "What did you hear?"

"Oh, nothing, really. A few twigs snapping, some leaves crunching. I even imagined I heard a growl." She waved her hand nervously. "I'm sure they're all natural out here in a small town. Guess I'm just a city girl."

Mac held still and lifted his face to the night. Not a breeze shifted the air. The atmosphere was dead calm. "No, your instinct was right. There's not enough wind to stir a leaf. Something was crawling around out here."

She shuddered. A half laugh escaped on a wisp of air, and she pressed her hand to her mouth. "Probably the neighbor's cat or something."

"Maybe." Mac didn't want to alarm her any more than he already had. He forced a smile to his face and tapped Joey's back. "Just to be on the safe side, let me walk you home."

"But what about your horse and Molly?"

"I've arranged for Daniel to bring my horse over on his way back to the ranch. He'll be along in a few minutes. Molly's around here somewhere." He whistled softly. Molly silently leaped out of the darkness to sit at Mac's feet.

Eve backed up another step. She laughed, but her laugh was more like a squeak. "Look at me, all jumpy."

"It's okay." He held out his hand for hers. "Come on, it's getting late."

Eve didn't protest. Slipping her hand in his, she held on.

Her fingers were cold at first, but eventually

warmed in his. Something about walking this way, holding Eve's hand and carrying Joey, felt right to Mac. Too right.

His life had been screwed up since the day his mother left him and his dad. He didn't have anything to offer this woman and her son. And she'd already said she didn't want to get involved in a relationship. Good thing. At least he knew where they stood.

Still, her hand felt good in his and when he'd held her close, she fit against him. Not too tall, not too short, she snuggled right below his chin. Perfect. Warm, sweet-smelling Eve. She could crawl right beneath his skin if he let her.

When they arrived at her doorstep, he promised himself he'd see her safely in and leave. No more mooning over something that wasn't meant to be. No lusting after a woman he shouldn't even be concerned with. He'd see her to her door and walk back to meet up with Daniel. How hard could that be?

He should be more focused on whatever could be skulking around the town of Spirit Canyon. Could have been any number of small animals. Raccoons, armadillos, opossums and skunks were regular visitors looking for the abandoned bowl of cat food or digging into un-protected trash. But what if the animal was something more dangerous? Something that had taken down a goat weighing roughly the same as Eve.

Had the print in Eve's yard been from the same creature that had killed his goat just over the hill? If so, it was bold enough to wander the streets of a populated area. Usually a wild animal avoided human contact. But once it learned of the easy pickings in a town, it became a deadly liability. What would it attack next? A pet? A tremor ran the length of his spine. Or a woman and her child?

AS MUCH AS SHE WANTED to be independent and never rely on a man's strength, Eve couldn't let go of Mac's calloused hand. His warmth seeped through her skin and chased away the chill of fear that had gripped her. She stole a sideways glance, noting how Joey slept on, secure in Mac's arms.

Eve's heart warmed at the sight. The man had already had an impact on Joey's life and, if she were honest with herself, on hers, too. Something about Mac's quiet strength eased her burden, made her feel safe.

When they reached her porch, she reluctantly let go of his hand to dig into her pocket for the key. The night air penetrated her sweater, causing her to shiver. Was it the night air, or that she'd let go of the warmth of Mac's hand?

Eve unlocked the door and reached in to switch on the porch light, dispelling any romantic notions. Then she inhaled deeply, plastered on a smile and faced Mac. "Thanks for seeing me home. I'll be sure to do my walking in broad daylight from now on. At least until I get used to the sounds that go bump in the night around here." She held out her arms for Joey.

Mac stared over her shoulder, his hands never budging from her son. "Why don't I take him to his room so we don't disturb him again?"

Hesitating for a moment, Eve stood blocking the door. Why didn't she just move aside and let him in? Allowing Mac to put her son to bed wasn't an invitation to take *her* to bed, too.

He'd have to take Joey into her bedroom, the only room she'd made habitable. The one she and Joey shared until she put the last coat of paint on the walls in his room.

She closed her eyes and mentally shook herself. She really needed to get a grip. The night was making her act crazy, imagining sounds that weren't there and actions Mac couldn't possibly be thinking.

Eve opened her eyes.

"I thought for a moment I'd lost you," he said. A smile played on his lips, softening the harsh lines around his eyes.

Mac standing there holding her son did funny things to Eve. It'd be best if she got Joey to bed and sent Mac on his way before she lost her resolve to keep this man at arm's length. "The bedroom is up the stairs, first door on the right."

With a nod, Mac slipped past her in the small hallway, his arm lightly brushing Eve's breast.

She flinched at the stimulating jolt that coursed through her.

Mac climbed the stairs effortlessly and entered the room.

Eve followed his tight jeans up the stairs. When she entered the room, she hung back, maintaining her distance, reminding herself of why they couldn't be together. Because her son was the only man she'd allow in her life until he was grown.

Mac eased Joey on the bed and pulled off his shoes and socks. Then he straightened and looked Eve in the eye. "Will you be all right alone?"

"Yes," she said with a little more force than she'd intended.

His gaze lingered, the blue-gray of his eyes darkening. "I'll be on my way. Don't forget to lock up behind me."

Then he was gone. Just like that. One moment he was dominating the room with masculine appeal, the next moment the room was empty, except for Eve and a sleeping Joey.

As she went through the routine of dressing her son in pajamas and tucking him into bed, her mind drifted back over the day. When she descended the stairs to lock the doors and check the windows, goose bumps rose on her arms. Not like anything would get in, she told herself. Animals couldn't open doors and windows, and all the people she'd met in Spirit Canyon were friendly—with the exception of Toby Rice. A chill crept down her spine, but she refused to dwell on the one snake in the grass. So what did she have to be afraid of when wrapped in the protection of her house?

Once dressed in her nightgown, Eve climbed into bed. When she leaned over to switch her light out, she held her breath.

A long, wailing sound echoed outside her window.

She strained her ears. The old house creaked and then the windows shook, blasted by a gust of wind.

Blowing out her breath, Eve switched off the light. If she weren't careful she'd get paranoid.

THE NIGHT AIR HUNG like a heavy blanket, thick with moisture from the clouds pressing around her. Why didn't it just rain? The ranchers needed the precious, life-giving moisture to keep their animals and crops from dying. And Eve needed to see the sunny day and moonlit night that were sure to follow. But there was no moon this night. The dark pushed against her chest, making it difficult to breathe as she walked through a thicket of stumpy live oak trees interspersed with the rangy mesquites. Why she was out at night, she didn't know. Hadn't she already learned that lesson? She didn't even remember getting out of her bed much less walking way into the woods. Where was she going? Where was Joey?

While questions tumbled in her mind, she kept walking. Then a bright orange glimmer of light appeared through the dense brush. Eve picked her way around the scrub cedar, ducking beneath the low-hanging branches of gnarled oak trees, to get to the light.

Almost there, she paused behind a stand of young cedar saplings. She'd heard voices. With a cautious hand, she pushed aside a branch blocking her view of a clearing.

The light came from a fire in the shape of a blazing ring. Around the circle of light stood a group of men all dressed in hooded black capes, all turned toward one man. He stepped into the ring of fire and lifted a white squirming creature high above his head. It was a baby lamb or goat. Its terrified bleating shattered the stillness. Then the man turned his back to where Eve stood. The bleating ceased and silence reigned.

Eve's heart banged against her chest, fear choking the air from her throat. What had happened to the baby animal? Why did it stop crying?

The man in the fire raised his hands above his head. Instead of the animal, he held a shiny metal chalice. "Hail, devourer of blood, who camest forth from the block of slaughter."

The ring of men shouted, "Hail!"

Eve gasped and pressed a hand over her mouth. Devourer of blood? What kind of heathen ritual had she stumbled upon?

"Hail to the spirit of the wolf, may he lead us to greatness!"

"Hail!"

"Now drink the blood of innocence. Drink to strength!" The leader lifted the goblet to his lips and drank. Then he passed through the fire and handed it to the next man, who drank. And around the circle the chalice traveled until it came to the last figure.

Eve sensed the evil emanating from this last man, more so than the leader of the ceremony.

He tipped the chalice and drained the last drop, then threw it into the flaming ring. The fire flared, momentarily blinding Eve.

The last man's voice rose above the crackling flame, not a shout, but a steady, mesmerizing tone, seeping into the minds of those people standing around the circle. "We have the strength of the wolf. We are the voice of the future. We will not be cowed by others who would rob us of our land and belongings. Stand strong. Stand together. Or suffer retribution. Stand strong. Stand together. Stand strong. Stand together."

Eve swayed toward that voice, swayed toward his thoughts, caught up like the others in his chant. Her lips moved to the words, until she realized what she was doing. She took an abrupt step backward, shocked at how completely she'd been drawn in. The man with the mesmerizing voice looked across the circle, as if he could see through the darkened stand of cedar, straight toward her. His eyes glowed an eerie red from the shadow of his hood.

She stifled a scream and turned to run.

EVE SAT UP in bed and stared around the strange room. Several frightening seconds passed before she realized she was in her house in Spirit

Canyon, and Joey was safely sleeping next to
her. With a deep breath, she willed her heart to
slow to normal, and she eased down next to Joey,
pulling him into her arms. She lay there with her
eyes wide open, afraid to go back to sleep.

*Please, God, don't let the nightmares start
again. Please.*

Chapter Five

Dust filtered in through the open windows of the pickup. Despite the dry earth, the overhanging clouds promised to make the day hot and sticky. Some were calling the extended warm weather an Indian summer. Mac called it a fire hazard. He'd woken on the wrong side of the bed and wasn't fit for company.

The unsettled feeling probably had to do with a lack of sleep. Thoughts of killer animals and one redheaded lady were all it took to keep the weeds tumbling through his brain and sleep evading his grasp.

Daniel turned the truck out onto the main road leading to Spirit Canyon. "Heard that Anton Friemann boy from Kendall County got caught at school threatening some of the younger kids. Found a key chain on his backpack with a satanic symbol on it."

Mac frowned. He despised bullies.

"Did you know Toby Rice has been hangin' around that boy?" Daniel said.

"Doesn't surprise me."

"Rumor has it, some of the local teens are conducting some kind of late-night shenanigans, besides the usual drinkin' and shootin'. More into the live sacrifices."

"Just what we need." Mac's brows furrowed deeper. "You think they're responsible for the missing livestock?"

Daniel shrugged. "Could be."

"I'll check with the sheriff."

The foreman turned the truck into Eve's driveway, jerking Mac back to his immediate problem. Eve.

Daniel let the truck glide to a stop and then shifted it into Park. "Once I replace the columns on the porch, I should be able to handle the rest without you."

"Good." Mac climbed from the truck, not at all contemplating the work ahead. Instead his thoughts were wrapped around the woman stepping out on the porch.

"Hello." Eve waved from the top step. Even though she was dressed in an old T-shirt and cutoff shorts, her impact poleaxed Mac.

When their gazes met, Mac couldn't look away for a very long moment. With a physical jerk, he turned to gather tools from the back of the truck. He needed to keep focused on the work to be done.

"I can't get over how hot it is already," Eve said. "You'd think with all the clouds, we'd get a reprieve."

"Sure could use a little of that moisture on the ground," Daniel said over his shoulder as he joined Mac, unloading saws and lumber. "Haven't had rain in the past sixty days."

"It's as if the sky is looming, waiting for something to happen." With hands tucked into her back pockets, Eve descended the steps and toed the bushes in the gardens bordering the house. "I'm gonna have to water these bushes to keep them alive." Dark circles beneath her eyes indicated more concern than was necessary for a bunch of dying plants.

Not that Mac should be noticing the smudges beneath her eyes or the way her hips swayed when she walked. He dumped the tools on the porch and strode back to the pickup for something heavy to exert himself. If Eve hung around while they worked, he'd probably end up nailing his thumb to the boards. Bracing his legs, he lifted a twelve-foot long, eight-by-eight treated post.

"If you'll wait, I'll help you with that,"

Daniel shouted from the porch where he'd bent to plug in the circular saw.

Mac's muscles strained and sweat popped out on his brow, but he didn't stop to wait for Daniel's help. Besides, the stress on his shoulders and back helped alleviate the Eve effect. By the time he tossed the board to the ground, he was back in control. Muscles screaming a little, but back in control.

Daniel walked by, his lips twisted in a sardonic smile. "Show-off," he said beneath his breath.

Another trip to the truck for an eighty-pound bag of concrete mix, and he didn't have any more reasons to walk away from the house and her. He squatted to lay the bag of concrete on the ground.

Not two feet in front of him was a pair of battered tennis shoes. As he straightened, his gaze traveled the length of a pair of mighty fine, creamy white legs.

"Have I offended you, Mr. McGuire?" Eve asked.

Allowing his gaze to continue its upward path, Mac skimmed over denim-clad hips. He swallowed, his mouth suddenly dry as the hard-packed soil. "No, not at all. Why?" His gaze finally rose to those troubled green eyes, sparkling like finely polished jade despite the hint of a frown creasing her forehead.

Eve gave him half a smile. "You haven't even said hello."

Mac moistened his lips. "Hello."

Her breasts heaved upward and she blew out a tiny puff of air and laughed. "Heard anything more on the animal attacks?"

"Not since yesterday." He didn't know enough about what Daniel had told him regarding the teenagers' activities to trouble her unnecessarily.

"Still think I should be concerned about Joey?" She worried her bottom lip.

"Yes." Unable to drag his gaze away from how her teeth chewed at that lip, Mac was startled by a knee-buckling force hitting his legs. He stumbled into Eve, grabbing hold of her shoulders to keep her from falling. For a moment, he stood with his mouth a breath away from hers and all he could think about was how those lips would feel against his. As soon as he steadied and was sure Eve wouldn't fall, Mac let go.

Eyes wide and her breath rasping in shallow, rapid puffs, Eve all but jumped backward. She looked like a doe trapped by a hungry wolf.

Joey clung to Mac's calves, then let loose and reached up.

A laugh bubbled up from Mac's throat, dispelling the pent-up breath wedged there. "Good morning, Joey." He swung the boy up into his arms and chucked him under the chin. "Gotta be careful sneakin' up on someone like that. If it had been anyone but me, he'd have turned you upside down, like this."

Mac gripped the boy's thigh with one hand and tipped him upside down.

Joey spilled sideways, dangling by Mac's one hand, giggling like a normal four-year-old.

The sound filled Mac's chest with an unexpected warmth. The giggle was the first happy noise he'd heard Joey make.

When he lowered the boy to the ground, Joey hopped up and down, reaching for Mac.

"Sorry, little man. I have work to do. But you can help." Mac walked over to the live oak tree in the front yard.

Joey followed so close behind that he bumped into Mac when he stopped.

Mac bent and selected a sturdy stick, broke it in half and handed it to the boy. "Molly needs some exercise. Would you mind throwing this stick for her? She'll bring it right back to you."

Joey pushed the stick back into Mac's hand and shook his head, backing away, searching the lawn for the dog.

"It's easy. Watch." Mac whistled.

Molly's head popped up over the rim of the

truck bed. In a flash, she leaped over the side and raced toward Mac.

Joey turned, poised to run.

Mac scooped him off the ground and held him high. "Whoa! Wait a minute there."

The boy buried his face against Mac's shoulder and tried to crawl higher up his chest.

"Hey, what's all this?" Mac pried Joey's arm loose from his neck and turned him to face Molly.

To her credit, Molly sat patiently staring up at the stick in Mac's hand. Her tongue lolled to the side and her stumpy tail jerked back and forth.

"Watch this." Mac slung the stick across the yard.

Molly was off in a flash, body streamlined, concentration centered on the stick. Snapping it up in her teeth, she raced back to Mac.

As the dog approached, Joey turned to hide his face in Mac's shoulder again.

"Good dog." Mac bent and slipped the stick from the dog's jaws. "Your turn."

Joey shook his head.

"No? I have so much work to do and Molly really likes to play fetch," Mac said. "Are you sure you won't play with her?"

Joey shook his head again.

"You here to help, or what?" Daniel called out good-naturedly.

Mac gave Molly a sad look. "Sorry, girl." Then he hurled the stick across the driveway and set Joey on the ground. "Daniel says I have to work." He walked away, stealing a backward glance.

Joey stood in the middle of the yard staring at the dog, who after retrieving the stick, raced back to Mac.

"Go on. I don't have time to play." He patted her head, purposely ignoring the stick she dropped at his feet. He joined Daniel and together they hoisted a two-by-four under the eaves of the porch overhang close to the rotted column. Once it was in place, Mac turned back to Joey.

He stood still in the middle of the yard.

Molly deposited the stick at his feet. When Joey didn't throw it, the dog leaned over and nudged the stick onto his foot.

Joey's eyes widened, but he didn't look away from the dog.

When he saw Eve took a hesitant step toward her son, Mac held out his hand. "Wait." He could tell she wanted to grab him up and shield him from his fear. But Joey had to do it himself.

The boy stood as if rooted to the spot.

Not to be thwarted, Molly emitted a soft *woof!*

Galvanized by the sound, Joey spun on his heels and raced for the porch and his mother's arms.

EVE SQUATTED to absorb the full brunt of Joey's pell-mell run to protection. She hugged, but stubbornly refused to lift him when he pushed against her. Joey had to get over his fear without his mother's coddling. "It's okay, Joey. Molly only wanted to play." She pulled him off her and turned him toward the yard.

Joey still clung to her arm, his fingers digging into her flesh.

Molly sat where Joey left her, the stick lying on the ground, her head tilted to one side.

"See? She's confused. She doesn't understand why you won't throw the stick."

Joey loosened his grip on Eve's arm, but remained between her knees.

"Don't you want to play with Molly?" she asked. When Joey shook his head, she stood and patted his backside. "Okay, then, why don't you go find some tracks, oh mighty hunter boy? We grown-ups have a lot of work to do."

She strode past the men, already working on the second post. "I'll be painting the back door, if anyone needs me."

As she walked around the side of the house, she couldn't help the warm, sunny feeling she had about Mac's attempt to get Joey over his fear of dogs. He didn't have to try. He wasn't in any way obligated to help her son. Which made it all the more poignant. For a damaged ex-soldier, he was good through and through, definitely a hard man to forget, especially when the remembered warmth of his hands on her shoulders still made her skin tingle. Good with her son and loaded with sex appeal, Mac was double trouble. Eve could fall in love with a guy like him.

With that thought troubling her mind, she rounded the hedge, the back steps coming into view. A creamy white animal lay sprawled across the landing.

Eve's heart thumped against her ribs. When she edged closer, she noticed the angry red streak splashed across the creature's pale neck.

A scream ripped from her throat and she staggered backward. Her breath labored in ragged gasps, and her blood pounded so hard against her ears, her vision swam.

When her knees buckled, two strong arms were there to catch her. One circled her shoulders and the other slipped beneath her thighs.

Mac scooped her up against his chest. "Daniel, grab the boy," he yelled over his shoulder.

As the fog cleared from her brain, Eve struggled against the arms holding her high above the ground. "Joey. I have to get to Joey."

"It's okay. He hasn't seen it. And Daniel will make sure he doesn't."

She glanced back at the bloody white mass of what once had been an innocent lamb, strewn across her back step. Bile burbled in her stomach and again she struggled. "Please, put me down," she said desperately.

Mac frowned. "I'm not sure that's such a good idea."

"If you don't, I can't be held responsible for the contents of my stomach." Her belly heaved and she fought to maintain control.

Mac dropped her legs, but his arm remained looped around her shoulders as he guided her into a bent position.

There, in front of God and Mac, Eve emptied her breakfast on the ground, tears streaming unchecked from her eyes.

Mac held onto her to keep her from collapsing. He brushed the hair behind her ears, whispering soothing words of comfort.

When she'd completed her purge, she straightened, but wouldn't look at Mac. "I'm sorry. It's just…I had a really bad dream last night and…" She stared at the innocent lamb. "And now this." How could she tell him about a dream that seemed to have come true? He'd probably think she'd lost her mind.

"Can you stand on your own?" His low voice was comforting.

"Yes. I think." She wrapped her arms across her stomach to ward off any further gastronomical theatrics.

He let go of her shoulders. "Here, let me." Grabbing the hem of his black T-shirt, he brushed the tears off her face and smoothed the hair away from her brow. "There, good as new."

Eve gazed up into eyes that reflected the steely gray sky. He'd been so kind, so gentle when she needed it most. Tears leaked again from the corner of her eyes. "I don't know what's wrong with me. I just can't help it."

Mac pulled her into his arms, laying her head against his chest.

And she wept full-fledged, soak-the-skin buckets of tears. Tears for Joey, tears for this man and his hidden scars, tears for the little lamb ripped to shreds and tears for the hell her life had been for the past six months.

When her eyes had emptied and nothing but hiccups remained, she sniffled, inhaling the scent of Mac. A pulsing ache built low in her belly—an ache that had nothing to do with tossing her cookies, and everything to do with being too close to Mac.

His hands had settled around her back,

rubbing her muscles in gentle circles, skimming over her spine and the waistband of her cutoffs.

Everywhere his hands touched her felt as if sizzling surges burned their way across her nerve endings. How could this be? Hadn't the carnage of an animal's death been enough to rein in her growing desire for this man? She tilted her head up to stare into his eyes.

A corner of his mouth quirked upward and he leaned over to kiss her forehead. "Go in through the front door. I'll take care of this before Joey has a chance to see it."

"Are you sure?" She didn't want to look again. The dream image of the terrified animal made her heart hurt. She was thankful Mac and Daniel had been there when she'd found the animal. She didn't think she could have faced the horror alone.

"Go inside." He turned her in his arms and gave her a little shove, sending her in the direction she'd come just a few short minutes earlier when her dream about a sacrificial lamb had only been a dream, not the nightmare of reality.

Berating herself because she already missed the warmth of Mac's arms, Eve tried to remember she wasn't on the hunt for a man in her life. As a painful reminder, a vision flashed into her mind. The one of her stepfather tossing her report card full of straight A's into the trash as he scolded her for putting his beer on the wrong shelf in the refrigerator. He'd never encouraged her or congratulated her for her hard work. The fact was, he never loved her. And Eve would be damned if she placed Joey in that position. Suddenly she wanted to see that her son was okay, hold him close and feel his living, breathing body beneath her fingertips.

SHOUTS SHOT THROUGH Mac's mind, shouts of pain from men struck by flying shrapnel. Harsh images spilled into his memories—the roadside bomb, the ambush following its explosion, blood spurting from wounds that would never heal. Everything had happened so fast, he could do nothing to protect his men.

When he'd seen Eve standing over the dead lamb, he could only send a prayer of thanks to God she was okay. Whether or not she would have collapsed, he didn't know. But he had to hold her to feel for himself she was still alive.

He'd maintained a facade of calm while he'd held her in his arms, projecting strength and protection. But as soon as she'd gone around the side of the house, Mac's entire body shook. Just like he did after every nightmare. He shouldn't still be shaking over the past. He was stronger than that, damn it!

Within minutes, Daniel joined Mac, carrying a shovel. "I thought—" He slammed the sharp end of the shovel into the earth. "Hell, I don't know what I thought when I heard her scream."

Mac clenched his fists to still the shaking in his hands and slow the hammering in his head and chest.

"You all right, Mac?" Daniel laid a palm against his shoulder.

The simple gesture of compassion sent a sudden burst of rage rifling through Mac, shooting adrenaline through his veins. "Yes," he answered a little more sharply than he intended.

"As long as you're okay." Daniel lifted the shovel and readied to scoop up the offensive mass.

"Don't." Mac grabbed his arm.

The foreman stared up at him, a perplexed frown creasing his brow. "Why not?"

"We need to know what killed the lamb. If we disturb the evidence, we will only delay the search."

With a sharp stab, Daniel dug the tip of the shovel into the ground. "You're right."

Squatting next to the dead lamb, his heart still racing, but back in control, Mac examined the body. "I've seen a lot of animal kills in my life, but this isn't one of them. This lamb was cut and drained of its blood."

Daniel scraped off his straw cowboy hat and scratched his head. "Sounds like maybe the rumors aren't just rumors. But why leave the dead body here on Ms. Baxter's back porch?"

"A warning?" Mac asked, his body tensing. Who would have a gripe against the new girl in town?

Daniel stood, brushed his hat against his thigh and jammed it back on his head. "Why here? Eve's one heck of a nice lady for someone to harass."

A sick knot cramped Mac's gut, as if he should dread something but he didn't quite know what that something was. He straightened next to Daniel and stared into his eyes. "I don't get it, either. And it doesn't explain the dead goat. That most definitely was an animal attack. I got a bad feeling Eve and Joey aren't safe here on the edge of town."

Daniel held Mac's gaze for several long seconds and nodded. "Yeah. So what are we gonna do about it?"

Before Mac could formulate a plan, he heard a honking sound from the front of the house. Mac, with Daniel close behind, loped around the side to see Sheriff Hodge's SUV idling in the driveway.

Eve, holding Joey in her arms, stood talking to the sheriff. Her face was pale and her eyes were still red and puffy.

Mac fought the sudden urge to go to her, take her and Joey into his arms and protect them from danger. He had no right to feel that way. To preserve his sanity, he tore his gaze from Eve, but the somber look on the sheriff's face didn't bode well.

"Mac, Daniel, sorry to disturb your work, but we need your help," he said in his deep Southern drawl.

"What's the problem, Sheriff?" Daniel asked.

"Had a couple more animals go missing last night." Sheriff Hodges glanced at Eve and Joey. "Ma'am, not sure you want the boy to hear this."

"I understand." Her gaze met Mac's. "Joey and I were just headed to the store to visit Ms. Addie, weren't we, sweetie?"

Joey wasn't listening, his gaze fixed on the lights twirling on top of the sheriff's Tahoe.

When Eve turned to leave, Mac laid a hand on her arm. "I'll remove the animal once the vet has had a chance to look at it."

Eve nodded and walked away.

"What animal?" Sheriff Hodges asked as soon as Eve left.

Mac watched Eve's vehicle until it disappeared down Main Street, then he turned to Sheriff Hodges and told him of Eve's discovery. "We just found the lamb a few minutes ago."

The lawman shook his head, his mouth pressing into a grim line. "That would account for one of the missing animals."

"What was the other?" Daniel asked.

"Mrs. Baumgartner's registered miniature stallion. The lamb was one of Mr. Frantzen's show lambs, taken right out of the pen next to his barn." Sheriff Hodges leaned in the window of his car and grabbed his handheld radio off the seat. "Shirley, call Dr. Herbst and have him come to the old Felton place?"

"The vet?" A female voice crackled over the radio.

"Yeah." The sheriff's mouth thinned into a line.

"Did you know there was a group of men gathering at the feed store?"

"Yeah, Shirley," he said tiredly. "Call over there and tell them to hold up until I get there." The sheriff hooked the radio onto his belt.

"What's this about men gathering at the feed store?" Mac asked.

"A group of ranchers want to go on an organized hunt on Frantzen's ranch to find the animal responsible for all the killin' going on around here. One of the guys has a couple huntin' dogs he swears can find a gnat on a flea if you get them on the scent."

"Is that why you came to find us?" Mac asked.

"Yup. Seein' as how your property borders Frantzen's, thought maybe you'd want to be involved."

Before Mac could reply, Daniel stepped forward. "Sure, Sheriff. Mac and I would love to help. We all have a stake in finding the killer."

Mac's gut tightened. The last time he'd been in a group of armed men, they'd all ended up dead. Not that this was the same situation. Still, a familiar sick feeling of dread filled him.

He stood there, staring down at the hard-packed earth. The ground was so dry, cracks a quarter inch wide spread in all directions. A strong wind gusted from the west across the hills, filling the air with the parched, earthy smell of dust and stinging the eyes with grit.

A feeling of déjà vu slipped over Mac's subconscious. Fallujah had been dry that day. Dry and dusty. Halfway around the world, the clouds blocking the sun had been a heavy layer of swirling sand. The kind that made a man wear a scarf over his mouth and nose so he could breathe. Sand that made him squint until he could only see through a narrow slit. Not enough to see his adversary until too late.

Once again, just as in Iraq, he was fighting an enemy he couldn't see.

Chapter Six

"Addie," Eve called out as soon as she entered the general store, Joey in tow. "What's going on down at the feed store? There are a lot of trucks crowding the parking lot."

"Howdy, Eve. I'll be with you in just a moment." Addie glanced up briefly while counting change into a customer's hands. "Thank you, Dottie. Sorry to hear about your horse."

"These things happen," Dottie said. "Just seems to be happenin' a lot lately." She gathered her purchases and exited, calling over her shoulder, "See you at church on Sunday!"

As Dottie left, Laura strode in carrying a box. "Eve, I'm so glad you came by. This is the second box of flyers back from printers. Cynthia was supposed to be here fifteen minutes ago to help fold, but as you can see, she isn't here. I could surely use an extra set of hands."

"I'd be happy to help," Eve answered. Perhaps by helping, she could get her mind off the lamb.

Laura smiled down at Joey. "And how are you today, young man? I left Katie playing hide-n-seek somewhere around here. Why don't you see if you can find her?"

Joey dropped Eve's hand and raced down the aisle.

"So what brings you and Joey out so early, Eve?" Addie asked, as she set to polishing the spotless wooden counter. "I expected you two to be workin' that old house until sunset. Weren't Daniel and Mac out there helpin' you?"

"Yes, but we were interrupted by a present left on my back porch and the sheriff showing up." Eve sat on a stool in front of the counter and leaned her elbow on the polished surface. "What's going on? I thought I found a quiet little town in the country."

"Normally it is." Laura lifted the lid from the box and set it aside. "What kind of present did you find on your porch?"

"A dead lamb." Eve shuddered. Red blood against the dingy white of the small lamb's wool was a vision she wasn't soon going to forget.

"Good Lord!" Addie exclaimed. "How the heck did something like that end up on your back porch?"

"Just the question I've been asking myself."

"Did Joey see it?" Laura whispered.

"No, thank God."

Laura glanced around the store till she saw the children.

"Relax. They're okay." Addie waved a hand. "They're havin' themselves a fine ol' time."

"More than I can say for the men." Laura's voice was tense. "They're organizing a hunt."

"A hunt?" Eve asked. "Is that why they're gathering at the feed store?"

"Yup. More animals have gone missin'." Addie sighed. "Ain't seen nothing like this in thirty years. Seems like history's repeatin' itself."

"You mean the story they were talking about last night?" Laura handed Eve a stack of flyers and the three women started folding. "That was really sad about Mac's mother."

"Sadder if you'd known her," Addie said. "She was as pretty as they come, with her shiny black hair and blue-gray eyes. Mac's got his mamma's eyes, but his dad's hair." She slid her finger along the paper, creasing it neatly. "Never a mean word out of that woman's mouth. She thought the sun rose and set on Frank and Mac."

"What really happened, Addie? Why did she run away?" Laura leaned her elbows on the counter. "I was helping old Mrs. Frantzen out this morning, and she said Mac's mother was raped by a monster. What was scary was I think Mrs. Frantzen actually believes it."

"No one really knows, but whatever happened to her was something she couldn't live with, and she couldn't let her family suffer. She wouldn't have left other than to spare Frank and little Mac." Addie's normally happy smile turned downward. "She loved them that much. I feel it in my bones that she left to save her husband and child from her torment."

"What could possibly have been so bad that the love of her family wouldn't help her get through it?" Eve couldn't imagine anything horrible enough to keep her from being there for Joey.

"Frank spoke of the nightmares Jenny had. She'd wake up in a cold sweat, sure that creature was coming back for her. Within a month, she'd lost weight, quit visitin' me here at the store and stayed in her house with the shades drawn. I went by to see her and she was still in bed, sickly like. I mentioned something to the doc. He said the strangest thing." Addie paused. "Said he'd done all he could for her, the rest was in God's hands. Not two days later she disappeared."

"Do you think she committed suicide?" Laura asked.

Addie shrugged. "Frank said she packed a bag and left a note for him and Mac. She said she loved them more than life, but not to follow her. Leavin' was something she had to do." The older woman brushed a tear from the corner of her eye.

Laura sniffed. "Poor Frank and Mac. It must have been awful losing her. And poor Jenny. I can't imagine leaving Katie."

A lump threatened to choke Eve's throat. All she could do was nod. How terrible to lose your mother at such a young age. Her heart wept for the young Mac. "Did they ever find the animal that attacked her?"

"No."

A chill shivered across Eve's skin. "You don't think it's the same creature that's harming the animals now, do you?"

"I can't imagine any creature capable of living for thirty years and still having the strength to bring down a full grown Boer goat." Addie stared up into Eve's eyes. "Come to think of it, I don't know of any animal that would purposely drop a 'present' on a doorstep. Sounds more like something a mean-spirited person would do."

"I had a cat who brought a mouse into my bed once." Laura grimaced. "It was as if she was proud of her kill and wanted to share it with us. I thought I'd have to burn those sheets to get the smell of dead mouse out of them."

Eve smiled weakly. "I can't quite burn my back porch to get rid of the memory of that poor little lamb." A shiver shook her frame.

"No, you can't. But that's what friends are for. To talk it out." Addie walked around from behind the counter and wrapped Eve in her arms. "Sometimes, all a body needs is a big hug."

"Hey, let me in on some of the action." Laura wrapped her arms around the two women. "Addie's right. When you need a friend, count us in."

Tears trickled down Eve's cheeks. "Thanks. You don't know how much this means to me." She hadn't felt this loved since before her mother died in a car wreck.

When Laura and Addie stepped back, they all laughed a little self-consciously and went back to work folding pamphlets.

The bell over the front door jangled as the door banged open. Cynthia hurried toward the back counter, her voice shaking. "I'm so sorry. I must have forgotten the time." A bluish-purple bruise marred her right cheekbone, in sharp contrast to her pale skin.

Eve gasped. "Good Lord! What happened to your face?"

The young girl blushed and ducked her head. "It's nothing. I hit the cabinet door putting dishes away last night."

Addie frowned, marched around the counter and grabbed the girl's shoulders.

Cynthia winced and shrank back.

The older woman's mouth pressed into a tighter line. "Did that hurt you when I touched your shoulder?" She stretched Cynthia's T-shirt over the shoulder, displaying yet another bruise. "And I suppose this bruise was from the same cabinet?"

Liquid pooled in Cynthia's eyes. "It's nothing, really."

"When you gonna stop coverin' for that no 'count boyfriend of yours?" Addie tipped Cynthia's face toward the light. "He hit you pretty hard. He ain't got no business beatin' up on a girl."

"It was my fault." Cynthia glanced at Eve and back down at her feet. "He was so mad when we left here last night."

Anger washed over Eve. "You mean he hit you because I told him to be nice and treat you with respect?"

"He was angry." Cynthia grabbed Eve's hands, gripping them until they hurt. "You won't say anything, will you? Please don't say anything to him. He swore he wouldn't do it again. He said he loves me."

Eve wanted to gag. What kind of man could hurt someone he professes to love? "Cynthia, if he really loved you, he wouldn't hurt you."

Tears poured down her cheeks. "He didn't mean to. He just got so angry. Toby really loves me. He said so."

"It's okay, honey. We won't do anything stupid." Eve pulled the woman-child into her arms and stroked her back the way she would stroke Joey. "It'll be okay." The entire time she held Cynthia, she fumed, fighting back the urge to run right out and take a two-by-four to Toby. Violence didn't cure violence. But what kind of animal could do this to such a nice girl? A mean-spirited person, that's who.

Eve raged at any abuse, having been the recipient of countless insults, derogatory remarks and mental flogging from her stepfather. She'd fought the torment by avoiding confrontation and retreating inward until she grew old enough to move out of her stepfather's house. What she couldn't understand was why a woman would tolerate physical abuse when the man didn't live in her house. With the girl held tightly in her arms, Eve vowed to do something to help Cynthia before Toby crushed her spirit completely.

"OVER BY THE RIVER on the Frantzen ranch, we found one of the missing lambs." The sheriff paused and looked around the men in the parking lot of the feed store. "And this time we got a trail. We need every man on the hunt to corner it."

"I'll donate a hundred dollars to the man who brings in the animal." Mayor Logan stood next to the sheriff, wearing khaki slacks and a polo shirt.

"Where's your rifle, Mayor?" Bernie Odom asked.

"I don't own one." The mayor shrugged and smiled. "Never had a need for one. Besides, I'll leave the hunting up to those with more experience."

The men headed out in a convoy of trucks and dust.

They'd found a trail. A temporary sense of relief washed over Mac, followed immediately by the question, what if it wasn't the right trail? And how were they supposed to see it in the dark? The sun was just dipping below the blanket of clouds, to merge with the horizon.

The Frantzen ranch bordered the McGuire acres on the north side with the river separating the two tracts of land.

Trucks littered the yard and horses, tied to the live oak and mesquite trees, shifted nervously in the dark. Half the men from the county stood with lanterns, shotguns, rifles and hunting knives gathered around Sheriff Hodges and Fredrick Frantzen. They talked in small groups, faces intent, their excitement permeating the air.

"Glad ya'll could make it." Sheriff Hodges nodded his greeting to the men. "Fred, you want to tell everyone what you found and where?"

"I was out in that dry gully just past the caliche pit, you know the one with the wild mulberry trees." He scrubbed his straw cowboy hat off his bald head and ran a hand across the few wisps of hair clinging to his scalp. "Anyway, I spotted one of the lambs I'd been missing since noon yesterday. Course, she was dead as a doornail."

"Will you hurry up, old man?" Toby groused. "Whatever it is will be long gone by the time you finish."

"Hold your tongue, Toby," Art Nantan said.

Toby stood in front of Art. "You gonna make me? You're always bossing me around. Well, I'm sick and tired of it."

"That's what bosses do. But we can fix that." Art planted his fists on his hips. "You're fired."

"Suits me fine. Didn't like workin' at that stinkin' feed store of yours anyway and sick of you always tellin' us what to do and how to do it. You think you're so great, but you're not. Someday one of the brothers is going to take you down. Just wait."

Art shot a look around the gathering crowd. "Shut up, Toby."

"No." The young man stood with his arms crossed over his chest, the sleeves of his dirty white T-shirt rolled up over his shoulder made him look like a gang member from the fifties.

"Someone needs to shut your mouth." Art's hands rose to chest level, his fists bunched into tight knots. "I might just be the one."

"Take him down, Art. That boy's got to learn his place," Jess Harding shouted. "Been beatin' up on my girl, he has."

"Yeah! Nail 'em to the dirt," Hank Bleumfeld yelled.

Toby stared across the packed dirt at Art, breathing like an angry bull about to charge. "Your time's up, old man. Even if I don't take you out, someone else will."

"You're a loose cannon, Toby. You don't know when to keep a lid on it. You're nothing but a punk who can't even control his temper." Art's words were like jabs. "So put up or shut up, punk."

With the speed of youth and the power of a

football lineman, Toby launched himself at Art, knocking the older man flat on his back.

Mac shook his head. What was wrong with these people? Not a one of the men standing around lifted a finger to stop the fight.

Mac strode up to the men rolling on the ground and, with one hand, yanked Toby up by his belt loop. "Enough!"

When Toby could no longer land punches on Art, he scrambled to get his feet under himself and started swinging at Mac.

Mac blocked each swing, the blows smarting against his arms, but not landing in his face or gut as intended. The hand-to-hand combat skills he'd learned in the Army came in handy.

Daniel slipped behind Toby and yanked his arms behind his back. "Settle down, kid."

"I'm not a punk and I'm not a kid." Toby breathed heavily, glaring from Art, who'd climbed to his feet and was brushing dust from his jeans, to Mac.

"I don't care what you are," Mac said. "We're here for a reason, and it's not to fight each other."

Toby snorted. "We're wastin' our time." He shook Daniel's grip loose and straightened. He snorted and snatched his cowboy hat off the ground, slapping it against his thigh.

Mac's eyes narrowed. "You seem mighty sure of that. Care to explain?"

"He's just a dumb kid. What does he know?" Art stood beside the sheriff. "Come on, boys, let Frantzen tell his story."

"That's right, put your differences aside and let the man speak," Mayor Logan said, his voice soothing, his ever-present smile friendly.

Frantzen glared at Toby and scratched his head again. "Now, where was I?"

Mac stifled a groan.

"You were out in the gully and found the lamb." Sheriff Hodges rolled his hand. "And?"

"Anyway, there's this spring back there that leaches out of the hillside and runs down to the river. That's where I found tracks and the lamb. Looked like hog tracks," Frantzen said. "Might be javelina or feral hogs, I don't know. Either one could be dangerous."

Javelina. Mac would bet his back teeth that whatever laid the lamb on Eve's back porch wasn't a javelina.

"I've hunted javelina before," Daniel said. "They can be very aggressive."

"Nothin' a little lead won't cure." Toby hefted his rifle.

"Just make your aim count," Sheriff Hodges said, shooting a narrow-eyed look at Toby.

"We won't be using the dogs, as they'll scare the hogs away before we get a shot off. Once we get to the gully, we're going in on foot." Sheriff Hodges turned in a circle as he spoke and stopped to single out Toby again. "Okay, men, it's already dark and there's not much in the way of moonlight. There's quite a few men out here so don't shoot unless you know what's on the other side of that bullet. You may have to take the animal out with nothing more than a knife to avoid hitting a man."

Mac stared around at the men, maybe fifteen in all and each one carrying a rifle. His chest tightened. If they did come across a herd of hogs, and everyone started shooting…

"Bring it on. I can handle it," Toby said. "The rest of you can stand around and talk. I'm gonna have ham hocks for supper." He started away from the group.

"Stick together or the animals may get past you," the sheriff urged. "We'll need to spread out in a line and move through the area, making a clean sweep. If you see anything, shout. These animals can cover a lot of miles in a short amount of time. We want to take it, or them, down so we don't lose any more livestock. Got it?"

"I can take about ten of you in the back of my pickup," Frantzen said.

"I'll take the rest in the back of mine," offered Bernie.

"You riding with me, Toby?" Frantzen asked.

"I'll take my own," Toby said. "I never ride in back."

"Suit yourself," Frantzen muttered.

Mac grabbed his rifle from his vehicle and climbed in the back of Bernie's truck next to Daniel. He felt for his hunting knife in the sheath at his waist.

As the truck rumbled over the rutted track toward the gully, the smell of diesel fuel shot Mac back in time to the HUMMVs he and his troops had been driving when the roadside bomb exploded beneath them. The first vehicle had been disabled, the men inside maimed or killed in the blast.

Mac's breathing grew shallow. He could still hear the echo of their cries.

Wounded by flying shrapnel and blocked by a crippled vehicle in the road, Mac and the rest of his men had been sitting ducks. Loyalists to Saddam Hussein fell on his squad, shooting and hacking away at those remaining. As if in a nightmare, Mac couldn't move, couldn't run to the rescue, couldn't stop those men from murdering his troops, his friends. His wounds immobilized him and within seconds he'd fallen unconscious, left for dead, the sounds of the enemies' cheers mocking him.

When the old farm truck hit a large rut, Mac was jolted out of his morose memories. They had arrived at the caliche pit. Bernie parked next to Frantzen, and men clambered down from the trucks, checked their weapons and spread out with twenty feet between each person.

Before everyone was in place, Toby snorted. "I'm not waitin'. I got me some bacon to bring home." He trotted off into the brush, swallowed by the dark.

"Great," Daniel said. "Now we can't shoot our rifles, 'cause we don't know where that idiot will be."

"Who says we can't shoot?" someone said in the shadows. "Could put more than one irritating animal out of our misery. One with a really big mouth."

Nervous chuckles worked their way down the line of men.

"Let's move out," Sheriff Hodges called out.

The human line moved deliberately through the hill country, down into the gully. They passed the point where the lamb lay mutilated beyond recognition. The earth had been rooted around and disturbed like only a hog could do.

Mac aimed his flashlight at the lamb and

shook his head. This lamb and the one left on Eve's doorstep didn't look the same. The one at the house had been neatly sliced and drained of blood. The one he stared at now had been torn apart and eaten. Its formerly white wool was trampled into a muddy, bloody mess. Not much left, kinda like the goat he'd found on his property. But he'd never heard of a feral hog taking down a hundred-and-twenty-pound goat. No. He had to admit this lamb and his goat had been attacked by animals. The lamb left on Eve's porch most likely was left by a human.

Mac recalled Toby's angry words with Eve at the community centre the previous evening. He knew Toby was nothing but a bully bent on intimidating others to make himself feel big. But was he capable of pulling such a cruel prank on the new girl in town?

Given Toby's track record of picking on schoolmates, and barroom fights, he probably would sink low enough to scare a woman. Would he frighten her enough to leave?

Mac didn't want Eve to leave. He couldn't put a name to his feelings, nor did he want to. For that matter, he shouldn't be having any feelings for her at all. His life was enough of a mess without dragging her into it.

The line of men moved on through the brush

in the direction of the tracks, careful to avoid stepping into the sharp needles of the prickly pear cactus. Progress was slow with clouds pressing in on them and no moonlight, only the beam of flashlights to guide them.

Not long after they'd passed the dead lamb, Mac heard gunshots and Toby screamed.

Every man broke the line and crashed through the brush in the direction of the noise.

Closest to the commotion, Mac held his rifle in front of him, hesitant to use it for fear of hitting Toby or one of the other men, instead of the hog.

He broke through a line of cedars into a small clearing. Several feral hogs surrounded a scrubby live oak tree, not much taller than a one-story house. Perched in the branches, hanging on for dear life, was Toby, bleeding from a wound in his thigh.

Some of the hogs spotted Mac, lost interest in Toby and charged the much more accessible target on the ground.

Outnumbered by at least seven to one, Mac stood firm with his rifle aimed at the closest hog. He hoped like hell Daniel, and the rest of the guys would get there soon and that some trigger-happy yahoo didn't shoot him in the backside.

"Shoot 'em!" Toby screamed from his roost in the tree.

Mac waited until the first hog was three feet away, aimed his rifle then pulled the trigger. The force of impact stopped the hog in its tracks, but the next one was only half a length behind the first. Mac fired again and dropped that one, too.

The five remaining hogs charged. Mac fired and heard answering gunshots join his. But one of the hogs he shot didn't stop when the bullet hit him. Its head dropped low, tusks aimed at Mac's knees.

Mac fired again, but the hog kept coming. "Are you just too stupid to die?" The third bullet, fired point-blank, took the beast down, but its momentum carried it forward to collapse against Mac's shins, knocking him to the ground. His rifle flew from his grip, landing a couple of yards away.

When Mac's head hit the ground, pinpoints of lights flittered through his vision. Heart thumping in his chest, he pushed up on his elbows, looking for the next barrage of hogs, only to discover the rest had scattered into the shadows.

Footsteps crashed through the underbrush and the men all gathered around, a cheer rising into the darkness.

"We're gonna have us a barbecue tomorrow night," shouted Bernie.

The thought of food turned Mac's stomach.

As he pushed the hog off his legs, his hands shook. He hadn't fired a shot in the past four months. But he didn't feel any better about killing animals than he had humans.

"Where's Toby?" Sheriff Hodges asked.

One flashlight was joined by others shining up the tree. Toby climbed down and held up his hand to block the lights.

"Hey, Toby, thanks for being the bait," Bernie called. "Sure helped the rest of us hunt those hogs."

Snickers erupted in the shadows.

Toby blustered, "I could have handled them if my gun hadn't jammed."

"Yeah, Toby," Art jeered. "Kinda hard to shoot when you're climbing a tree at the same time."

"Screw you." Toby grabbed his rifle from the ground and limped back the way he'd come.

Daniel appeared in front of Mac and stretched out a hand. "You all right?"

Mac clasped the proffered hand and allowed Daniel to help him to his feet. "Yeah." He brushed the dust off his jeans and searched the ground for his Stetson.

"That was a close call." Daniel handed him the hat and hooked his thumbs in his belt loops. "I'd hate to think you survived Iraq only to be bulldozed by a feral hog."

Mac stared around at the dead animals. "Seems a waste."

"What are you talking about?" Daniel shone the light into Mac's face. "You must have knocked your head on a rock. Don't you understand? We got 'em."

"Got what? A herd of feral hogs is all I see."

"We got the animals responsible for the missing livestock."

"I'm not so sure we did."

"How can you not be sure?" Daniel moved closer, speaking in low tones. "You saw the dead lamb back there in the gully. What more proof do you need?"

"The lamb we saw back there doesn't even compare to the one on Eve's back porch. A person killed that lamb. I'm sure of it. And not one of these hogs could have taken that Boer goat."

Daniel opened his mouth, shut it and scratched his head. "You got a point. I don't have to like it, but you got a point."

"Believe me, I wish I didn't. But my gut tells me there's something else out there."

"Well, time will tell." Daniel pulled out his knife and knelt in the dirt beside the still warm body of an ugly gray hog. "For now, let's field-strip and load up these animals for a trip to the packer. No use wasting good meat." He paused with his knife ready to start the job. "Hey, what's this?" He trained his flashlight on the ground to a wide, dark line in the normally light-colored soil.

Mac squatted next to him and scooped up a handful of black dirt. It felt like fine powder. He lifted it to his nose and sniffed. The acrid smell of burned mesquite assaulted his nostrils.

While the other men were loading the hogs onto their trucks and laughing about Toby's scare, Mac stood with Daniel shining his flashlight around a large ring of ash.

Chapter Seven

By the time she went to bed, Eve hadn't heard from Addie or any of the men who'd gone on the hunt. She worried about Mac outside on a dark night, with an animal known to kill small livestock still on the loose. If it felt cornered, would the creature go after grown men?

Shivers rippled throughout Eve's body. She tried to convince herself she cared only because Mac had been such a good influence on Joey. Unfortunately she cared for more reasons than his kindness toward her son.

When she finally closed her eyes, she drifted into a fitful sleep, already dreading the dreams she knew would come....

POISED ON THE EDGE of a rocky hillside, Eve stood in the silvery light of the night sky. Why was she here? Why now? Darkness and shadows swirled around the edges of giant boulders creating the illusion of gaping black maws beneath canopies of gnarled live oak trees.

A child's frightened cry sounded below her. Joey, his pale skin glowing blue in the moonlight, ran across a grassy meadow as fast as his little feet could carry him. Stalking through the underbrush behind him was a man. One moment he was walking upright. The next moment, the man dropped to all fours. Only, he wasn't a man. He was a wolf the size of a small horse.

Eve's chest tightened, fear lodging in her throat. "Joey!" she screamed, but the sound was whipped away by a blustery wind.

The wolf crept closer, his lips pulled back exposing long white fangs.

"No!" Eve scrambled down the hill, sliding on the loose gravel, waving her arms and shouting, "No! Not Joey! Take me!"

Her shouts caught the wolf's attention and he leveled his cold blue gaze on her.

Fear for her child, compounded with fear for her own life, forced Eve to a skidding halt. She changed directions, leading the wolf away from her son. As if running through a pit of glue, she moved one frightening step at a time, dragging herself farther away. The heat of the wolf's breath bore down on her neck but Eve fought to put distance between her and the predator, the predator and her son.

She ran down the hill into the river valley. Her lungs near bursting, she stopped to catch her breath and look back.

The wolf had disappeared.

Oh, thank God.

With her hands braced on her knees, Eve hauled in huge gulps of air, until she could almost breathe normally again. Then she heard the sound. A deep hum of chanting.

Drawn through the woods, she followed the noise until it grew louder. Through a stand of scrub cedar, she could see a bright orange light. With one hand, she pushed aside the curtain of prickly cedar branches, pungent sap sticking to her fingers.

The light was a blazing ring of fire, the center of which was the size of a house, and empty. Standing in a circle around the blaze were men in hooded capes, chanting in a low, steady rhythm. The chanting grew louder, then suddenly ceased.

As one, the participants turned to face one man at the head of the group. He stepped into the center of the fire and raised his hand high. "Hail devourers of blood! Meet your new leader!"

Then Mac, in his ever-present black Stetson,

appeared inside the ring of fire and stood face-to-face with the caped figure. The chanting rose up around the two in the circle until the sound echoed against the trees.

"No, Mac!" Eve tried to scream, but she couldn't be heard over the roar of the other voices. She stood riveted to the ground, unable to stop him. Unable to save him from the evil.

Mac sliced his hand through the air and the chanting stopped. "We've had enough of you and your cult," Mac said. "I'm here to put an end to it."

"Not before I put an end to you!" the leader cried. Then he whipped the hood off his head, revealing the face of a wolf. The same wolf that had chased Eve only moments before.

With the light of the full moon shimmering off his silvery fur, he tipped his snout to the sky and howled a long, keening wail.

The sound filled the meadow, permeating the night, assailing Eve's senses until she could stand it no longer.

EVE SAT UP straight in bed, gasping for air, her pulse hammering so loud in her ears she couldn't hear. Had the howling been just a dream? Had she really heard a wolf?

Trembling all over from the horror of her

nightmare, she forced herself to lie back against the pillow until her heart rate calmed. At a time like this, she regretted not having a man in her lonely bed. What she wouldn't give to have someone lying beside her, to hold her tight and chase away her nightmares. If Mac were there, he'd protect her and Joey from real and imagined enemies.

But Mac wasn't there. What would she do if an animal attacked her or her son? Beat it off with a broom? For the first time since Joey was born, Eve wished she had a gun.

LATER THAT MORNING, after the sun had risen, Eve and Joey walked to the General Store. Joey went for the candy, Eve intended to follow through with the purchase of a gun.

Addie was sweeping the front porch as Eve and Joey arrived. "Good morning, sunshine!" The older woman tousled Joey's hair and smiled at Eve. "There's a Fruit Roll-Up on the counter in there just for you, Joey. Why don't you go find it?"

Joey dashed into the store without a backward glance.

"You're sure in a cheerful mood this morning." Eve found Addie's smile contagious and the corners of her lips quirked upward, helping to dispel the shadows of her sleepless night.

"Got every right to be." Addie made one last swipe at the porch with her broom, as if sweeping every one of her troubles away. "Didn't you hear?"

"Hear what?"

"They got 'em," Addie said. "They got the critters that have been killing the local livestock."

A flood of relief swept over Eve. "Thank God."

"Amen."

"Was it a wolf?" Eve asked, imagining the creature from her dream, relief washing over her like a spring shower.

"No. Not a wolf." Addie propped a fist on her hip and leaned on the broom. "They cornered a herd of wild hogs out on Freddie Frantzen's place. The hogs had just taken another of Freddie's lambs and left a slew of tracks for them to follow. Got about seven of the vermin."

"Sounds dangerous. Was anyone hurt?" Eve held her breath. Mac had been on that hunt.

"Surprisingly they had only one injury."

Eve's heart thumped against her chest, and she laid a hand on the woman's arm. "Addie, who was injured?"

"Don't worry your pretty head. There weren't any major injuries. Mac got knocked on his fanny."

Eve felt as if she'd been punched in the belly. Mac had been hurt?

"But he was right as rain when he came back from the hunt early this morning. A little sore, but on his feet." Addie crossed her arms over her chest. "Now, Toby Rice was an entirely different story. He shot himself in the leg trying to skinny up a tree. The boys won't let him live it down for a while."

Recalling the bruises on Cynthia's face, Eve couldn't think of a more deserving person. "I hope it taught him a lesson."

"More than likely just made him mad." Addie pulled a rag from her pocket and swiped at the bench set against the outside wall. "We should watch out for our Miss Cynthia. We need to keep her too busy to go out with that loser. He's liable to take out his anger on her."

"I could use some help cleaning the house," Eve suggested. Having Cynthia around would be refreshing, especially to know she wasn't around that jerk, Toby. "Think she'd be interested?"

"I'll bet she would. She only works part-time at the feed store. That's a right good idea. If I see her today, I'll send her by."

"Thanks," Eve said.

"So what brings you in so early?"

"I needed more cleaning supplies." She stared

through the screen door to make sure Joey wasn't within earshot. "And I had thought about getting a gun, but I guess I don't need one now."

"Get one," a deep voice rumbled behind her.

Eve's stomach flip-flopped and she swung around to stare up into Mac's blue-gray eyes. The relief of seeing him after worrying all night almost made her throw her arms around his neck. Thank goodness she had more control over her instinctive reactions.

Mac tipped his hat at both women. "Hello, Ms. Addie. Eve."

"I hear you guys took care of the animal problem." His nearness was causing strange reactions in her belly. Perhaps standing so close to Mac wasn't such a good idea. "Why should I get a gun now?"

Mac's lips tightened. "You live on the edge of a small town. Like I said before, wild animals don't always know the boundaries." Eve sensed he wanted to say more, but he didn't.

"Makes sense. But I don't know the first thing about shooting a gun, much less buying one."

"I got a couple of nine millimeter pistols, rifles and shotguns in stock, and I could order anything you like," Addie said. "But Mac's the expert, if you want to know which one's right for you."

Mac removed his black Stetson and ran a

hand through his dark brown hair, the bluish-purple circles beneath his eyes reflecting a tough night with little sleep.

"You must be exhausted," Eve said softly. "We could look at the guns another time. And, really, since the danger is no longer imminent, we don't have to do this at all."

With a sigh, Mac gazed down into her eyes. "No. A gun is a good idea. I'll come by later with some of mine. Once you've had a chance to fire them, you can decide which one works best for you. Then Addie can fix you up."

"If you're sure you don't mind." Eve half hoped he'd renege. Having Mac around confused her.

"I'll be there." He jammed his cowboy hat back on his head. "Daniel wanted you to know he'll be by later than usual today."

"Bet he wanted to sleep in after the hunt." Addie frowned. "I'm surprised you didn't. You doin' all right after last night's tumble?"

"I'm fine."

Addie slid an arm around Mac's waist and hugged him close. "I can't speak for the whole community, but thanks for taking care of those hogs."

Mac frowned and opened his mouth to say something, but before he could, someone else spoke first.

"Well, as the elected representative, I can speak for the entire community." Clint Logan stepped up on the porch, his gray suit and crisp white shirt as neat and tailored as Mac's jeans and black T-shirt weren't. "Thanks, Mac, for helping take care of a problem that's been plaguing the town and surrounding ranches. Why, you're practically a hero. I know I'll sleep better knowing that herd of wild hogs isn't roaming through the countryside. As a matter of fact, I owe you a hundred dollars." Clint flipped open his wallet.

"Keep your money," Mac bit out.

"I insist. I promised one hundred dollars to the man who could bring down the animal that's been terrorizing our community. I should really pay you five hundred, since you killed five hogs." The mayor smiled and held out a crisp hundred-dollar bill.

Mac's lips firmed into a straight line and a twitch jerked the side of his jaw. He glanced down at his cowboy boots. When he looked up again, he gazed straight into Eve's eyes. "I'll see you later."

"If you won't accept my money, at least accept my thanks for making this community a safer place," Clint said.

"Amen!" Addie said.

Without turning to acknowledge the other man, Mac stepped off the porch and strode toward the feed barn.

"What's got into that boy?" Addie's gaze followed him. Her eyes narrowed almost imperceptibly when she looked back to Clint. "Well, I don't have time to be lollygaggin'. Nice to see you, Mayor." She opened the screen door and turned to Eve. "How about those cleaning supplies?"

"I'll be just a minute. I wanted to ask Mayor Logan a question."

"What can I do for you, Eve?" Clint asked when Addie had gone inside. "You don't mind if I call you Eve, do you?"

"No, that's fine." Her gaze followed Mac as he entered the feed store. "So the men really took care of the problem animals?"

"That's right. A whole herd of hogs. Even found a dead lamb nearby." The mayor smiled. "We'll have a big barbecue to celebrate."

Eve didn't feel much like celebrating. If the mayor was convinced they'd gotten the right animals, why had Mac insisted on her buying a gun? "What did you mean by Mac being a hero?"

Clint's brows dropped a fraction and his lips pressed together. The movement was fleeting and his smile was back, firmly in place.

"Our Mr. McGuire walked right into the middle of the herd and started shooting. From what the boys said, about seven of them charged him at once. He got three before one knocked him on his backside. Took out two more from flat on his back."

A vision of Mac outnumbered by giant feral hogs turned Eve's stomach.

Clint slid an arm around her shoulders. "Don't you worry. He's a tough guy. And, as you noticed, he survived."

"Were you there?" she asked.

"No. I prefer hunting people." He smiled, tempering the words. "You know, in the courtroom." He turned her away from the store, ushering her down the steps. "Let me buy you lunch and we can talk the legalities of marketing your investment."

Eve ducked under his arm and stepped away. "No, thank you. I have work to do. Maybe another time." *Just not in this lifetime.* "Goodbye, Mayor Logan." She'd hoped the guy would get the hint that she wasn't interested. Eve hurried into the store to Joey and Addie, the unsettling feel of Clint Logan's arm on her shoulders lingering like the smell of wet dog.

He smiled as if he cared, said all the right words, but Eve didn't feel comfortable around him. What happened to trusting people? Had all the scary things happening in Spirit Canyon made her punchy?

MAC PULLED UP in Eve's driveway after noon that day. The mercury had climbed to the mid-nineties. He swiped an arm across his damp forehead. As hot as the air was, black clouds still lingered. For the past week, his mood had matched the sky. On the verge of erupting into something big, possibly violent.

Earlier, he'd let Clint Logan get to him. Mac didn't much care for the man. Who the hell was he anyway? In the five years Clint had been in town, he'd gone from being a stranger to a man with far too much influence. The townsfolk trusted and respected him. Why, then, couldn't Mac?

Perhaps the way the mayor hung around Eve had a little to do with Mac's aversion to him.

He'd come home to settle into a quiet existence, lick his wounds. Instead he found himself just as unsettled and on edge as he'd been since Fallujah. His hands fisted on top of the steering wheel.

As soon as he showed Eve how to fire a gun, he wanted to get back out to the Franzten place and check out that circle of ash in the daylight.

The burn mark worried him. It hadn't been the typical residue from a campfire or even a brush-burning pile. The ashes had been in a large circle with no sign of burning in the middle. Besides, anyone who'd start a fire in the hill country during a drought was foolish. But this was different. It had the smell of something more than burning brush or roasting weenies.

He climbed down from the truck.

The woman most prevalent on his mind stepped out on the porch wearing cutoffs and a T-shirt. Dressed as she was and wearing no makeup, she still knocked him back a step or two.

What was wrong with him? Strange things were happening in his hometown and he couldn't quit thinking about Eve Baxter. He couldn't help the overwhelming thought that she made Spirit Canyon feel more like home with her sweet skin and the love she obviously felt for Joey.

She descended the porch steps and walked halfway across the yard. "Joey's over at Katie's house. Laura picked him up a couple hours ago. I didn't want to worry about him while we were shooting. Hopefully he won't be back too soon." Her words came out in a rush and she twisted a trailing string on her shorts.

As if suddenly aware of his stare, Eve

dropped the string and rubbed at a streak of dark green paint on the back of her hand. "I just finished painting the back door. Guess I got more on me than the door."

Her light chuckle warmed Mac's insides.

"Need some help?" she asked.

As if her softly spoken words slapped him upside the head, he spun back toward the truck, grabbed a couple boxes of bullets and held them out. "If you'll carry these, I'll carry the pistols."

He stacked the boxes in her hands, his fingertips grazing the ribbed knit of the fabric covering her breasts.

Maybe coming here without Daniel was a mistake. At least with his foreman, he had an excuse to stay clear of the woman. Now, with Joey gone to the neighbor's house, Mac was alone and completely vulnerable to his rising obsession.

When Eve turned and walked toward the rear of the house, Mac grabbed the two weapons from the truck seat and followed her swaying hips. The cool, hard plastic of the grips against his heated palms did nothing to provide relief from the late-summer heat nor did it temper the raging blood flowing through his body.

"I thought we could set up in the shade of the

oak tree, to avoid getting too hot." Eve spoke over her shoulder.

Too late. His body was already a raging inferno and the rear view she was treating him to only stoked the furnace. He almost marched back to the truck, got in and drove away from temptation. A 440 engine might be the only thing that could get him away fast enough.

Eve chose that moment to turn. "I know you don't particularly want to spend an afternoon training an amateur how to fire a gun." She smiled. "But I really appreciate it."

How could he leave now? She was all sweetness and beauty; he'd be a fool to run. Hell, he'd be a fool to stay.

He stayed.

Laying the 38-caliber revolver and the 9 mm pistol on the ground, Mac relieved Eve of her boxes of bullets and placed them in the grass by the guns.

"I've never done anything like this before." Eve gave a little nervous laugh. "So bear with me."

"No problem." Other than wanting to forget about the guns, take her in his arms and kiss her long and hard, as hard as she was making him. "We'll start with loading the weapons." He lifted the revolver and popped the cylinder out to the side. "Just like in the old westerns, you fill each chamber with bullets. Make sure you point the bullets in the direction you want them to go."

He handed her the bullets and the gun.

She loaded the revolver, then stared up into his eyes, hers round and green with a smile crinkling the corners. "Now what?"

That smile had him shaking in his cowboy boots with the amount of restraint he had to exert to keep from yanking her into his arms.

He reached out and closed his hand around hers, shoving the cylinder back in place on the pistol. "Your pistol is loaded. It is now a dangerous weapon. Keep the safety on any time you don't plan to use it."

He reached around her other side and flipped on the safety. A light floral scent drifted up from her hair, teasing his senses.

Eve tipped her head back a little, drew in a long breath and let it out. "I see." Her voice cracked. She cleared her throat and said, "So, now all I have to do is point and pull the trigger?"

Mac stepped back, Eve's warmth and tantalizing scent clouding his brain. "While the weapon is on safe, get a feel for how it rests in your palm. You're right-handed, aren't you?" He really didn't know much about her. But what he did know made him nuts.

"Like this?" She lightly held the pistol in her

hand and curled her finger around the trigger. "And you're sure it won't go off?"

He smiled. "Absolutely. As long as the safety is on, you're safe."

"I don't feel so safe." Her words were muttered softly.

Mac had to lean closer to catch them. "You will once you feel more comfortable firing it." He spoke next to her ear and watched her shoulder quiver. His body responded by sending electrical shock waves along his nerve endings. "Hold the pistol steady by cupping your left hand under your right." He demonstrated with his hands.

"Like this?" Eve raised the weapon as he'd shown.

"Yes." Being close to Eve was wearing at his ability to keep his hands to himself. The sooner he got this lesson over with, the better. "Now, aim at that stump over there, cock the hammer back and switch off the safety."

Eve clicked the safety switch off. "Okay."

"Hold the pistol with your right hand, brace your left hand under it and sight down the barrel." His voice lowered. "Now, pretend that stump is attacking Joey."

Eve jerked the trigger. The shot went wide of the stump, raising a tuft of dirt twenty feet to the right of her target. She glared back at him. "Warn me next time."

He chuckled. "That's the point. You have to be prepared for the unexpected and fire with confidence and deadly precision. Your lives could depend on it."

"Now you're scaring me." Eve lifted her hands again and they shook slightly.

Mac raised his arms around her, fitting her backside to his torso, every cell in his body flowing like molten lava down a steep slope to pool at his loins. Why couldn't he leave her alone? Anger mixed with desire, forcing blood to pound in his ears.

Eve leaned back against him, her hair tickling his chin. Her eyes were closed, her breathing shallow and erratic. The hand holding the gun wobbled.

"Your life depends on your aim." Mac breathed into her ear. "Now, aim and fire."

She opened her eyes and took aim, and this time the shot hit dead-on.

"I did it!" She smiled back at him, her green eyes sparkling.

"Yes, you did." Mac took the pistol, flicked the safety and tossed it gently to the ground. Then he turned her in his arms. "And don't ever be afraid to shoot if something or someone is attacking you or Joey." His hands gripped her shoulders tightly. "Do you understand?"

She stared up at him, her eyes wide. "Yes, Mac, I do."

When her tongue ran across her bottom lip, Mac lost the tenuous hold on his control. "I didn't come here for this, but I can't help myself." His mouth crashed down on hers, and he filled himself with the taste of her lips and her tongue.

One hand cupped the back of her head, threading through the mass of auburn hair to the tender skin at the nape. His other hand ran down her back, lower still to the faded denim of her cutoffs. Sliding his hand into her back pocket, he snuggled her firmly to him, his arousal pushing hard against her stomach.

Eve's breath caught and her eyes widened, then the lids drooped low. She returned fire with an attack of her own, nipping at his bottom lip, pushing her tongue past his teeth to spar with his.

Their kiss was anything but gentle. Passionate and a little angry, but not gentle.

Mac couldn't get enough of her. Only naked and buried to the hilt would satisfy him with Eve. But even then he knew he'd want more. She wasn't a one-night stand. She was well and truly under his skin. And he damn well didn't need that. Nor did she.

Reason battled with desire and finally won.

Mac grabbed Eve's shoulders and shoved her to arm's length.

Her eyes, cloudy with desire, stared up at his, her brows pushing downward.

"We shouldn't be doing this." Mac's words completely contradicted what his body was telling him.

Eve stepped back until Mac's hands dropped from her shoulders. Her gaze crisscrossed over the yard and out toward the field leading to his ranch. She hugged her arms around herself as if suddenly cold in the heat of the late-afternoon sun. "You're right. We could never have a real relationship."

His eyes narrowed. "Why, Eve?"

"I love my son, and because I do, he will always come first." She stared up at him, her heartstrings tugging at the handsome face creased in a concerned frown. "Joey's happiness means more to me than my own life. I won't force another man into his life."

"And why would a relationship with a man jeopardize Joey's happiness?"

"Look, I lived with a stepfather. I know what it feels like to be on the outside looking in, to want so badly to be loved and never quite measuring up."

"Eve." He took her hands in his and then lifted her chin until he could see into her eyes. "I'm not your stepfather. Nor am I Joey's."

"No," she said staring directly into his face, "you're not."

And you never will be. Eve didn't say the words, but Mac could feel them like a blow to his gut. He felt as if he was the person on the outside looking in. And he didn't like it one little bit.

She glanced at the guns on the ground at their feet. "Maybe you should go."

A car door slammed at the front of the house.

"That will be Joey." Eve shot a quick look up into Mac's eyes and hurried around him.

He caught her arm. "Eve."

She stopped but refused to look up.

He didn't want her to leave, but what could he say? I screwed up? I was wrong? He couldn't, not when holding her had been the only right feeling he'd had since Iraq. When his lips touched hers, he'd come home. Not the white picket fence home, but back to a feeling, living and desiring kind of home. She made him feel alive again.

"I have to go," she said and shook her arm loose from his grip. She strode around the corner of the house, out of sight.

Her scent lingered on his mind and clung to his clothes. Would he ever be able to wash her out of his existence? Probably not. But for her sake and his, he had to try.

Chapter Eight

Eve fought for breath and calm. The short walk from the backyard to the front drive wasn't nearly long enough to erase the effects of Mac's kiss. A jog around the entire town of Spirit Canyon wouldn't be long enough.

She pressed a hand to her mouth and laughed softly. It was either laugh or cry.

Why did he have to go and kiss her? Damn it!

She paused behind the spindly branches of an overgrown crepe myrtle and breathed deeply. Then plastering a smile on her face, she walked around to the front yard.

Laura's minivan was parked next to Mac's truck in the driveway. The two children were already halfway across the yard, staring down at the dirt, obviously looking for tracks.

Laura glanced at Mac's truck and back to Eve, an eyebrow hitching upward. "I hope I didn't come back too soon. How did the shooting lessons go?"

The blood rushed up Eve's neck into her face before she could say a word. Damn, why couldn't she act normal instead of freshly kissed?

A grin spread across Laura's lips, and her eyes twinkled. "That well, huh?"

With tears welling in her eyes, Eve pressed her palms to her burning cheeks. The bombardment of emotions left her confused, embarrassed and scared. "No, not well at all."

"Hey, wait a minute there." Laura held open her arms. "Come tell me all about it."

"I can't." Out the corner of her watery eyes, Eve saw Mac stride around the house, pistols in his hands.

As soon as Joey spotted the man, he jumped up and raced toward him, hitting him at knee-level with a kid-sized bear hug.

Mac held the pistols and boxes of bullets out of reach. "Whoa, partner. Hang on a minute until I can put some of this stuff down."

Laura patted Eve's arm and whispered, "I'll get him." She hurried across the yard and peeled Joey's arms from around Mac's legs. "Let the man walk, sweetie."

Unencumbered by the four-year-old, Mac continued toward his pickup, depositing his burden in the front seat. Then he turned and squatted low to the ground. "Now let's have that hug."

Joey flew into his arms and squeezed him tight around the neck.

What was with her son? Eve experienced a momentary stab of jealousy. Had he swapped loyalties from his mother to this man he'd only known a short time?

She couldn't be mad at him or at Mac. Well, maybe for the earth-shattering, life-altering kiss Mac had given her. But not for befriending her son.

Another truck rumbled down the gravel driveway, pulling in behind Mac's.

Eve almost jumped in front of it and waved frantically to the other side of the driveway. But she couldn't just run out and say, *Don't block the driveway. Mac really needs to leave before I do something stupid, like fall in love with him.*

Daniel climbed down, rounded the hood to the passenger's door and opened it. "Hello, Eve. Addie asked me to bring Cynthia out. Said you might need some help inside."

Cynthia climbed down from the truck, clad in blue denim capris and a soft pink T-shirt. She looked like a little girl, except for the bruise on her face. Her smile was hesitant, her chin tucked low.

"Oh, good. I do need help." Relief flooded Eve, not for the added help but for the distraction Cynthia presented. Rather than dwelling on her issues with Mac, Eve could focus on the young woman-child.

While Cynthia crossed the yard to join the women, Daniel walked to the back of the truck. "Sorry I'm late." He called out over his shoulder. "I was plum tuckered after last night. Not as young as I used to be."

Molly leaped out onto the ground and ran to Mac.

Eve's heart slammed against her chest, and her first instinct was to lunge the three yards to Joey and snatch him up before Molly got to him.

But in one fluid movement, Mac straightened from his squatting position, lifting Joey away from the dog. "Hello, girl." He reached down and patted Molly's head. "Go find me a stick. Go on."

Molly raced away from Mac, her nose skimming the ground.

Joey's gaze never left the animal, but he didn't tense up like he usually did.

Having Mac and Molly around seemed to be helping Joey over his fear of dogs. How could she keep Mac away when his influence was having such a positive effect? At least Joey no longer went completely ballistic around the animal.

"Mac, glad you're still here." Daniel walked over to Mac and Joey, pulling gloves onto his hands. "I could use your help unloading and then we need to make that run to Johnson City for fencing supplies. Do you mind giving me a hand?"

Mac stared over at Eve as if asking her permission.

Her gut wanted to yell, Leave! But how fair was that to Daniel, who could use Mac's help? Instead, she nodded.

Mac set Joey on the ground and helped Daniel unload the truck.

While the men worked, Molly found a stick and returned to where Joey now stood alone. Without hesitating, the animal dropped the stick at his feet.

Eve held her breath, her heart skipping several beats as she waited for her son's response to the dog's invitation.

Joey stared at the stick, and then he glanced up at Eve.

She wanted to encourage him to throw the stick, but it had to be Joey's choice. Before he could see that she was watching him, Eve turned toward Laura and Cynthia. "How about a glass of lemonade?"

"Lemonade sounds fabulous," Laura said, and they turned toward the house.

Out of the corner of her eye, Eve saw Joey looking at her and back at the dog. *Please, Joey, play with her.* She wanted so badly for her son to live without fear, to laugh and play like a normal four-year-old.

Katie had made her way to the flower beds. When the little girl glanced up from chrysanthemums she'd been sniffing, she spotted Molly. "Ooooo! I want to play with the doggie." She raced across the yard as fast as her little legs could take her.

Before Katie reached him, Joey bent over, grabbed the stick and flung it.

Molly took off, catching the stick before it hit the dirt.

Katie jumped up and down and squealed, clapping her hands together. "Do it again! Do it again!"

Molly retrieved the stick and laid it at Joey's feet. This time the boy didn't hesitate. He lifted the stick and slung it across the yard.

Eve clutched Laura's arm, joy welling up with the tears in her eyes. "Do you see that?"

Laura nodded, covering Eve's hand with her own.

A smile stretched across Eve's face. She felt as if the sun was shining down on Spirit Canyon, Joey and her for the first time since they'd arrived. "Let's go get that lemonade." She linked arms with Laura and Cynthia, and they entered the house.

All confusion and fears temporarily receded in the simple delight of watching her son throw a stick for one mottle-colored dog. Perhaps soon she would hear the sweet sound of his voice again. Her son was on the mend, and everything else would work out. She was certain. MAC WAS STANDING next to Daniel by the truck when Joey threw the stick.

Eve's eyes and smile lit the yard. She really loved the kid and would do anything for him. Just like a mother was supposed to.

Not like his, thank God. Eve would never leave her son. Joey had enough troubles stacked against him. The love and support of his mother would help see him through. And Eve continuously proved her love for her son. She'd set aside her own needs and desires to ensure her son's happiness. Was it fair for Mac to want to be a part of her love and family?

"Cynthia's a nice girl." Daniel stared after the women. "Sure hate to see her hooked up with Toby."

Mac dragged his mind away from Eve to process Daniel's words. "Toby's bad for that girl. He's too hot tempered, out of control."

"Yeah." Daniel scuffed his boot in the dirt. "You see the bruise on her cheek?"

"Yes, sir." He'd seen Cynthia's face. The bruises made his blood boil. After the abuses he'd witnessed in Iraq, his stomach turned at the thought. Toby had to weigh at least twice what Cynthia did. "A man has no right to hit a woman."

"We need to pay that boy a visit."

"Seems so."

Daniel joined him by the tailgate. "What do you make of that ring of ash we saw last night?"

"Nothing's making sense." Mac ticked off his fingers. "The lamb at Frantzen's place looked like it had been killed by that herd of hogs, I'll give them that. From what the sheriff said, the miniature horse, like our Boer goat, had deep bite wounds like a large animal with long, sharp teeth killed it."

"Can't imagine a hog taking down a minia-ture horse, though," Daniel said.

"The lamb left on Eve's porch was clearly killed by someone with a knife."

"Yeah." Daniel scratched his jaw. "Sounds like we got us more than one problem."

"I'm thinking we need to check out that cult." Mac unlatched the tailgate and let it down. "I've heard of those kinds of groups conducting rituals using live animal sacrifices."

"That would explain the missing lambs and baby goats, but what about our breeder goat and the horse?"

"We need to keep our minds open to the possibility of a different kind of animal." Mac's lips tightened. "What I'm afraid of is that with everyone thinking the problem is taken care of, they won't be watchin' out for the little ones."

"Those other attacks were at night. Most folks don't let their little ones out after dark."

"True. But we've got the Harvest Festival coming up and the dance is at night." Mac nodded across at Katie and Joey. "And what if the animal is rabid? If it is, it would come out day or night and people wouldn't scare it off. But if this situation has something to do with the cult, what better opportunity to snatch more sacrificial lambs than when everyone's attention is on the party?"

Katie squealed and raced around the back of the house, Joey tight on her heels. Molly brought up the rear.

The sounds of children playing warmed Mac's heart simultaneously chilling it. He'd always wanted a yard full of kids, but he'd never thought he could stay in one place long enough to make a good father. When his father died, he couldn't stand living on the ranch without family. Daniel was there, but old ghosts made it painful. After his father died, Mac went to college and then straight into the Army to avoid his past and the sorrow of a ranch without his family.

When he was halfway across the world, buried in sand and blood, he'd finally figured it out. The old cliché, "Home is where the heart is" was so right. He'd never have a home as long as he didn't find someone to share it. His men had helped him to see that. When they were away from their families, they'd turned to each other. They were family.

Until they'd all been wiped out in an ambush. Everyone except him. A dull ache throbbed behind the scar on his forehead. He hadn't been able to save his father from pining away for his mother. He hadn't been able to save his troops from a roadside bomb and an attack by Iraqi insurgents. What the hell good would he be as a father to a boy like Joey or a husband to a woman like Eve?

Hauling concrete blocks made Mac's muscles burn and sweat poured into his eyes, taking his mind off other burning needs. Physical labor always grounded him.

When he was almost back in control and thinking he could escape without further incident, wild barking erupted from the backyard.

A child screamed.

Mac dropped the brick he'd been carrying, grabbed the .38 off his truck seat and tore around the side of the house, slamming bullets into the chamber as he ran. All the talk about rabid animals raced to the forefront of his mind.

Katie stood on the porch screaming at the top of her lungs.

In the middle of the backyard, Joey was rooted to the ground, his eyes as round as silver dollars, his face ghostly white.

Braced on all fours, her front paws spread wide, Molly snarled and barked at Joey.

When the boy saw Mac, he tried to step around Molly.

The animal wouldn't let him move. She growled and snapped at him without making contact, her barking continued.

Laura flung through the door and grabbed Katie. The little girl's screams died down into wet sobs as she buried her face in her mother's shoulder.

"Oh my God!" Eve leaped from the back porch, her face as pale as Joey's. She grabbed the broom off the stoop and raced across the yard. "Leave him alone!"

Before she got near the dog and boy, Mac lunged for her and grabbed her around the waist, trapping her arms against her sides. "Don't go any farther."

"Let me go!" She struggled against his grip, kicking him in the shins.

"Be still or the boy might get hurt."

"She'll kill him. Let me go!" Eve bucked and fought to get free.

Mac held tight. "Molly won't hurt him. She only barks like that when something's wrong." He scanned the ground around the dog and boy and spotted what looked like a dull gray, black and brown rock. The rock moved, emitting a rattling sound. "Rattlesnake."

Eve quit fighting and stood stock-still. "What should I do?" Her warm body trembled.

"Talk to Joey." Much as he enjoyed the feel of her body against his, Mac set her aside and aimed the 38-caliber pistol in his other hand.

"Joey, stay perfectly still, honey." Eve's voice wobbled, but she stared at her son until he locked gazes with hers.

Joey's gaze beseeched her to pick him up and carry him away, his eyes filling with tears.

The snake shifted inspiring another round of barking from the dog.

Joey cringed but remained still.

"Molly, quiet!" Mac commanded.

Molly stopped barking in midyelp. She looked at Mac, then down at the snake and growled.

"I know the snake's there." Mac's voice went from commanding to soothing. He needed the dog and the boy to remain motionless in order for him to kill the snake without hurting either one of them. "Good girl, Molly. Stay." He glanced at the petrified boy and smiled gently. "I need you to stand like a statue, Joey. Don't move a muscle."

"It's okay, Joey," Eve said. "Do like he says and be really still. Mac will take care of the snake."

Mac inched closer to make sure his bullet hit dead on with no chance of ricocheting off a stone and nicking the boy or dog. When he was in range, he cocked the hammer back and smiled at Eve, the irony of the earlier thwarted lesson not lost on him. "I hope you're paying attention. You may have to do this some day."

"God, I hope not." She shot him a weak smile. "Okay, Joey, close your eyes." Eve closed her eyes too and stuffed her fingers in her ears.

He didn't like to fire weapons near children, but Mac couldn't see any other way around it. He tightened his finger on the trigger.

The loud report shattered the silence and the snake bounced off the ground. Mac waited to see if it would move again. It didn't. "He's dead."

At Mac's quiet words, Joey rushed forward like water from a broken dam. Skirting the dog and the rattlesnake, he flung himself at Mac.

Mac bent low and scooped him into his arms. The boy clung so tightly around his neck he could barely catch a breath. "Not so tight, buddy."

Joey loosened his grip a little, but kept on hugging, tears streaming down his face.

"Are you okay, Joey?" Eve moved closer, laying a hand on her son's back. "Want to come to Mommy?"

The boy shook his head and clung tighter to Mac.

"It's okay. Mac saved you." Eve buried her face against her son's shirt, tears welling in her eyes.

With two crying people in front of him, Mac did the most natural thing he could. He wrapped his arms around Eve and Joey and hugged them close.

Daniel cleared his throat. When the hugging didn't break up, he began whistling tunelessly.

Eve backed away and scrubbed at her wet cheeks with her palms. "I don't know what came over me."

"I'd say you had yourself a little scare." With Katie perched on one hip, Laura crossed the yard and draped an arm around Eve. "Come on, let's go inside and have some of that lemonade we never got to."

Eve turned to Joey. "Come on, son. I'd just as soon you came inside with me."

Mac squatted and set the boy on his feet. But instead of going with his mother, Joey inched toward the snake and nudged it with the toe of his leather cowboy boot.

When the snake didn't budge, he turned to the dog. Molly sat quietly a few steps away, her tongue lolling out the side of her mouth.

"Molly saved your life, Joey," Eve said softly. She knelt next to the animal, looped an arm around her neck and hugged. "Thank you, Molly."

Molly turned to Eve and slurped her chin with a long, drooling swipe of her tongue.

Eve jerked back and laughed, rubbing the moisture from her face with the back of her hand.

"That's her way of saying you're welcome." Mac extended a hand to Eve.

She laid her hand in his and he pulled her to her feet.

"Thanks, Mac." She leaned up on her toes and pressed a kiss to Mac's cheek, and then she grabbed Joey up in her arms and strode to the house without a backward glance.

"If I had known all I had to do was kill one rangy ol' rattlesnake to get a girl to kiss me, I'd

have killed a whole passel of 'em by now."
Daniel thumped Mac on the back. "Think she's
got a hankerin' for you, son."

"She was just grateful."

"Grateful, my foot." Daniel grinned, and then
his face turned serious. "By the way, decent shot."

"Thanks." Mac leaned down to pat Molly's
head. "Good girl." The spot on Mac's cheek
where Eve had kissed him still tingled. Daniel
had gotten it all wrong. Eve didn't have a thing
for him. She'd have kissed a goat if it had saved
her son's life. Hadn't she hugged the dog?

He rubbed his cheek. Too bad they didn't
have a future. A man could get used to kisses
like that. But she'd made herself pretty clear.
She wasn't interested in bringing another man
into her and Joey's life.

Mac shook his head. Just as well. He didn't
want to be that man. He had issues of his own
to deal with. Then why couldn't he shake the
feeling those two needed taking care of? And
why did he keep visualizing Joey running
around his ranch, and Eve gracing one of the
wooden rocking chairs on his porch?

"Hey, what's this?" Daniel called out from
behind a large oak tree. He stepped out carrying
a burlap sack. "Haven't seen one of these since
they started selling feed in paper bags."

Mac took the bag from Daniel, opened it and sniffed. Besides the dry musty scent of burlap, he caught the strong stench of animal droppings only a scared and angry snake could leave. He shoved the bag away from him in a hurry, dread filling his belly. "That snake didn't just wander into the yard." He stared across at Daniel.

"I was afraid of that." Daniel sighed, his face grim. "Guess on our way to Johnson City for fencing supplies, we're gonna be stopping by to look at ashes and ask a few questions now, aren't we?"

Mac glanced at the dead snake. "You guess right."

Chapter Nine

Once her heart settled down in her chest and Joey was off playing somewhere in the house with Katie, Eve managed a long, steady breath.

"You okay?" Laura asked, sliding an arm around Eve's waist.

For a moment, Eve leaned on the other woman until she forced out a shaky laugh. "I live in Texas, for heaven's sake. You'd think a snake wouldn't have this big an effect on me."

"There's snakes, and there's rattlesnakes." Laura hugged her and let her go. "Me personally, I don't like any snake and would have reacted the same way if Katie had been the one cornered. My pulse rate is just now slowing to normal."

"Excuse me, Ms. Baxter." Cynthia cleared her throat, her face flushing pink. "I'm really glad Joey's okay."

Eve started at the sound of the teenager's

voice. "Oh, Cynthia. I'm sorry. In all the chaos, I completely forgot you'd come."

"Oh, that's okay." She shuffled her feet. "Where would you like me to begin?"

With a glance around the kitchen, her mind completely incapable of settling on one thing, Eve said the first thing she could think of. "Would you mind making the lemonade?"

"I don't mind."

Eve grabbed a can of frozen lemonade from the freezer and a glass pitcher from a cabinet, setting them on the counter. "I can't believe how much I'm still shaking."

Cynthia stepped up beside her and said quietly, "Go sit. I'll do this."

Eve collapsed at the kitchen table. "Okay. But only for a moment. I need to do something to get my mind off the snake." Not to mention the man whose kisses scared the fool out of her and all the other scary things going on in Spirit Canyon.

"Speaking of snakes," Laura said, staring straight at Cynthia. "Are you still dating Toby?"

The girl's hand stilled in midstir. "Yes, ma'am."

"Why?" Laura asked.

Eve stared at her new friend. Man, she didn't pull any punches, did she?

The teenager shrugged, her sweet face closing off, her lips pinching together. "I don't know."

"That you don't know tells me you've thought about leaving him." Eve rested a hand on Cynthia's arm. "Are you afraid he'll hurt you?"

The girl's chin dropped to her chest. "You don't understand," she said, her voice only a whisper. "It's all gotten so complicated."

Eve pushed all her earlier worries aside and grabbed Cynthia's hand. "Does it have to do with the cult?"

Cynthia's head jerked up, her eyes rounded. "What cult?"

"Don't be silly, Cynthia, we've heard all about the cult Toby runs with." Laura moved to stand in front of Cynthia. "Has he dragged you into it, too?"

"I don't know what you're talking about." She backed up a step, leaving the wooden spoon in the pitcher, twirling around.

Her hand falling from Cynthia's arm, Eve twisted her fingers together. "What do you know about the cult, Cynthia?" she asked softly.

"Nothing." The girl shook her head, tears welling in her eyes. "Nothing."

"I think you know a lot more than you're telling us." Laura reached out, palms up. "You can trust us, Cynthia. We just want to help."

"You don't understand." Cynthia pressed her

hands to her reddened cheeks. "You couldn't understand."

"Try us." Eve's heart went out to the distraught girl. She must be in real trouble if she was afraid to leave Toby, afraid of the cult.

"No one can understand. I can't leave them. I can't!" She spun around and darted for the door.

.Eve would have run after Cynthia, but Laura stopped her with a hand on her arm.

"Don't. She needs time to come to reason. Time to think about our offer of help."

"Laura, I'm not so sure she has time." Images of a ring of fire and men chanting filled Eve's head. Everything in her dream had felt so frighteningly real, as if it had already happened.

"What do you mean?" Laura clasped Eve's hands in hers.

"I had a dream about a cult last night. It was frightening and all so real."

A frown pushed Laura's eyebrows together. "But, Eve, it was just a dream."

"I know. I know." Yet, deep in her gut, Eve felt the dream had more to do with reality.

"I'll talk to Cynthia's father," Laura said. "Maybe he can talk sense into her."

"Okay. But do it soon, will you?" Eve added silently, *before it's too late for Cynthia.*

MAC KICKED at the loose dirt in the open field where they'd found the feral hogs. Where they'd seen the ring of ashes the night before was now neatly brushed dust. No signs of ash, nor the footprints they should have seen from the dozen or so men who'd helped clear the mess from the hogs.

"Someone covered their tracks." Mac pushed his cowboy hat to the back of his head.

Daniel chewed on a toothpick. "I'm not liking this."

"I think that cult is probably more of a reality than a rumor." Mac turned toward the truck. "Come on. Let's go talk to the sheriff."

Before the two men had taken more than two steps, a loud bang echoed off the hills.

"Get down!" Mac yelled. He dove for the ground and rolled toward the pickup.

Daniel hit the dirt and crawled for the relative safety of the truck's tire. "What the heck was that?"

His lips pressed into a firm line as he eased the driver's door open and reached behind the seat for his rifle. "That, my friend, was a gunshot."

Another shot shattered the rear window, spraying glass all through the interior of the truck. Mac covered his face and, rifle in hand, dropped out of the truck back to the ground.

"As far as I can tell, he's up on that hill on the

other side of the clearing," Daniel said. He crouched low behind the front wheel, peering around to catch a glimpse of their attacker.

Another shot pinged against the side door of the ranch vehicle.

"I just cleaned this darned truck," Daniel grumbled. "This guy is starting to make me mad."

"About to take care of him." Mac crawled beneath the pickup and positioned himself next to the rear wheel on the opposite side. A quick scan concluded nothing. "Hey, Dan," he said loud enough so that only the foreman could hear him. "Wave your hat over the top of the truck."

"Gotcha."

Mac heard scrambling in the gravel behind him and the next moment another shot rang out.

"Blast!" Daniel said. "He shot a hole plumb through my favorite hat."

That was when Mac saw movement from behind a thick green juniper tree. He sighted down the barrel of his rifle and squeezed the trigger. The sound exploded in the tight confines beneath the pickup.

For a moment everything was silent and still. Mac detected a slight movement from the hillside. Then what sounded like a motorcycle engine flared to life. A cloud of caliche dust obscured Mac's vision of the all-terrain vehicle that climbed to the top of the hill and disappeared over the ridgeline.

Mac pulled himself out from beneath the truck and stared at the dissipating dust. "Apparently our attacker didn't expect us to shoot back."

"Probably scared the piss out of him." Daniel joined Mac and turned to look at the damage caused by the gunman. "Look at this mess."

Mac patted Daniel on the back. "Think on the bright side."

"You mean there is one?"

Mac poked his finger at the hole in the door of the truck. "Better the truck than one of us."

"You make a good point." Daniel opened the door and used his holey hat to brush glass off the seat. "I'm thinkin' it's time to visit the sheriff."

"I have to agree." Past time, as far as Mac was concerned. A dead lamb was one thing. A rattlesnake and bullets were an entirely different story. One he'd like to see have a happy ending.

"I'LL HAVE THESE casings sent to the state crime lab ASAP." Sheriff Hodges slipped the metal bullet casings into a plastic bag and handed them to his deputy. "Now, what were you two doing out at the Frantzen place that made someone mad enough to shoot at you?"

"We saw a burned circle there last night after

the hog hunt and wanted to come back to see what it was all about in the daylight."

"And?" The sheriff took up a tablet and pen and jotted notes onto it.

Daniel chimed in. "Someone came back before we could and covered any signs of the burn."

Sheriff Hodges looked up. "I'll have a talk with Frantzen."

"We stopped on the way here. Frantzen swore he didn't know a thing about it and didn't see anyone drive out there. With over six hundred acres of hill country, anyone could have come in from one of his other gates and left without him ever knowing it."

"You're right. But I've had other reports of burn circles on local ranches."

"You have?" Mac asked.

"Yeah. Never could catch them in the act."

Mac paced in front of the sheriff's desk. "Any pattern to the locations?"

"Not really. Only the out-of-the-way places like Frantzen's."

Mac stopped in front of the sheriff. "Any idea who might be involved?"

"I've heard rumors, but nothing concrete. That group is tight-lipped. Real tight."

"I think they're the ones responsible for the

dead lamb on Eve's porch. And today we found a live rattlesnake. At first I thought it just wandered in, like they do sometimes. But Daniel found a gunnysack nearby."

"So? The wind could have brought it in." The sheriff looked unfazed.

"Not smellin' like snake poop," Daniel added from his position leaning against the doorjamb.

Sheriff Hodges shook his head. "But why Ms. Baxter? She's only been here a couple days."

"All I could think was that she stood up to Toby Rice in public." Mac recalled the fire in her eyes when she'd told Toby to let Cynthia go. He almost smiled at the memory. Except her actions had caused an even greater negative reaction on Toby's part. "My bet is that he's a member of that cult. He could also have been the one shooting at us. I believe he owns an ATV."

With a nod, the sheriff tucked his pad beneath his arm and his pen his shirt pocket. "I'll start there. At the very least, it'll make him think twice before pulling any more stunts, knowing the law is onto him."

The sheriff climbed into his SUV and headed out of town on Main Street, straight for Toby Rice's house.

"Are we still going for those supplies or do

we wait until tomorrow?" Daniel asked. "What do you want to do?"

"I just want the threats to stop. That woman and her kid don't deserve to live in fear." Neither did Mac want to worry about them, but he couldn't help it.

As they made their way to the truck, Mac said, "Maybe we should check at the feed store and see if they have what we need in stock. That way we can ask some questions of the folks Toby worked with. Maybe they know something about the cult activities."

"You're the boss." Daniel climbed behind the wheel. "Let's go."

Chapter Ten

"Addie, have you seen Cynthia?" Eve and Joey strode into the General Store at four o'clock that afternoon. After sanding the hallway floors and painting Joey's room, Eve couldn't stand it anymore. She needed to know Cynthia was all right.

Addie looked up from talking to Bernie Odom and tucked her hands in the pockets of her shop apron. "Nope. Can't say that I have. I thought she was out at your place."

Eve sighed. "She was until Laura and I scared her off."

"I can't imagine a pretty thing like you scarin' anyone." Bernie turned and smiled at her.

"Thanks, Mr. Odom. Laura and I mentioned the cult we've been hearing rumor of and she took off."

With a shake of her gray head, Addie clucked her tongue. "I was afraid of that. I bet Toby

Rice got her into whatever trouble he's been playing with."

"Yeah." With a sigh, Eve slid onto a stool at the counter and leaned her chin on her fist. "That's where the conversation started. For that matter, that's where it ended."

"Seems like every time we've had a really bad bout of weather, like the drought we're havin', where crops and livestock die, folks get all wound up. That's when you hear more about that danged ol' cult that's been around for as long as I can remember," Bernie said.

"What did you say?" Eve sat straight and stared at the older man. But before he could explain, Addie spoke.

"We had a drought around seven years ago." Addie crossed her arms over her chest, a frown pulling her brows low over her eyes. "Did you hear about the cults then?"

"That one wasn't so bad." Bernie scratched the day-old whiskers on his chin. "No, I'm talkin' about the kind of drought that cost a lot of ranchers their places. You know the one. When Nantan, Adams, Harding and Bleumfeld lost all their cattle. They plumb starved to death. We went four months without a single drop of rain."

"I remember that." Addie stared across the

store as if she were looking into the past. "That's about the time Jenny McGuire disappeared."

Eve gasped. "You think the cult had anything to do with Jenny disappearing?"

"I don't think so." Bernie shook his head. "By all accounts, she left on her own."

"What kind of cult is this, anyway?" Eve asked. "One of those satanic cults where the worship the devil?"

"No. From the rumors that flew around back in Jenny's day, I heard it was something to do with wolves."

The wolf in her dream. All the air rushed out of Eve's lungs. Without oxygen to her brain, fuzzy gray crept in around her peripheral vision.

"You all right, Eve?" Addie asked. "Your face is all white."

Bernie's arm hooked around her shoulders. "Maybe you should lie down somewhere."

The desperation in the old man's voice broke through Eve's trance and she inhaled. "I'm sorry." A few more oxygen-rich breaths and her vision cleared. "Must have breathed too many paint fumes this afternoon in Joey's room."

"Why don't I walk you and Joey home?" Addie said.

Eve forced a shaky smile to her lips. "No, no. I'm okay."

"Well, look. I gotta go." Bernie backed toward the door. "Stock to feed, and all that."

Eve almost laughed out loud at how quickly Bernie released responsibility to Addie. As if the thought of a woman passing out in front of him made him shake in his boots.

"You know, Eve, I think we should do our homework on this cult thing." Addie removed her apron and laid it over the counter. "Come around to the back. Let's see what we can find on the Internet."

"Joey, come with me." Eve grabbed Joey's hand and pulled him behind the counter with her, afraid to let him out of her sight.

A half hour later Eve sat next to Addie, her head swimming with the overload of information found on the Internet. Everything from Indian wolf worshippers to werewolf cults of Europe. Only one recurring theme reverberated in her head. She pointed at a phrase on the screen. "There."

"Yes, that's what I keep seeing," Addie said.

Eve read aloud. "We travel alone—wolves in sheep's clothing until we come together where we can be as family. The wolf is the teacher, pathfinder on the never ending journey of survival; strong in character, tenacious, the symbol of family."

"A cult is where folks who don't have a sense of belonging find a family."

Eve snorted. "A sick family."

Addie nodded. "But a family, nonetheless."

"But why here in Spirit Canyon? This is such a tight community." Eve rose from her chair and paced around the little office at the back of the store. "The people seem to look out for each other."

"Yeah, but when hard times come, some draw closer while others push away."

"What do you mean?" Eve asked.

"The dry spell we had thirty years ago caused rifts between the ranchers who kept their ranches and those who lost them."

"You think they still hold grudges?"

"Hard to tell. All that wolves-in-sheep's-clothing stuff. Who knows?" Addie logged off and sat back. "Makes you wonder who your real friends and enemies are."

Eve wished she could laugh it off, but the image of the wolf chasing first Joey, then herself through the hills was too recent. Too real. All she wanted was to go back to her house and lock all the doors.

But Eve knew, even with the doors closed and locked, she wouldn't feel safe. The truth was that she only felt safe when Mac was there with them.

WHEN THEY ENTERED the feed store, Mac decided to hang back several steps, since Daniel had been around Spirit Canyon a lot longer than he had lately. Folks were usually more willing to share with someone they knew well.

"Howdy, Dan. Mac. What can I get for you today?" Hank Bleumfeld stood behind the counter, a friendly smile on his face.

Dan fished around in his pocket and dug out a toothpick. He'd given up smoking two months ago, but anytime he was nervous, he still reached for the cigarettes. "Could use five hundred feet of thirty-six-inch field fence and fence staples if you got them," Dan said around the toothpick.

"Let me see if we have it in stock." Hank punched keys on the computer behind the counter. "Can't help you with the fence to-day…it's on back order. But got the nails."

"Guess I'll have to head to Johnson City for the fence."

"If you can wait, we can have it here in a week."

"No, I need it tomorrow. That old Brahma bull took out a section of fence yesterday and if I don't get it back up soon, he could be halfway to Dallas before you know it."

"Is there anything else I can help you with?"

"As a matter of fact there is. Have you seen

Toby?" Daniel took the toothpick out of his mouth and waited for Hank's response.

Hank Bleumfeld's gaze shifted from Daniel to Mac and back. "You remember what happened last night. Art fired him—and he meant it."

"Any idea what caused that fight?" Daniel asked, leaning against the counter like he was there to chew the fat.

Hank's gaze shifted again. "Nope."

Daniel smiled at Hank and pushed the toothpick aside to say, "You've lived here all your life, just like me, right?"

"Yeah." The man behind the counter stretched the one word out as if buying time to figure out where Daniel was going with the question.

"Heck, we went to the same school growing up."

"Sure did," Hank said. "Only you were a year or two behind me, if I recall."

Mac shifted, impatient for Daniel to get to the point. But he held his tongue, knowing Daniel would eventually get there and Hank wouldn't know what hit him when Daniel did.

"I bet working here, you hear all the gossip for the county and surrounding towns, huh?" Daniel twirled the toothpick on his tongue.

"I suppose so." Hank's eyes narrowed.

"Then maybe you can you tell me if you've

heard anything about cult activities happening in the area?"

Bingo. Daniel nailed him with the question Mac would have asked at the outset of the conversation.

For a moment, Hank's eyes rounded and he appeared a little off-kilter. If Mac hadn't been watching closely, he'd have missed the slight evidence of surprise, because Hank reverted quickly to a blank face, his gaze dropping to the cash register. "Don't know what yer talkin' about."

"Really?" Daniel crossed his feet at his booted ankles. "And I thought you knew everything there is to know about the people around here."

"Some things a man doesn't need to learn about," Hank grumbled. "If you don't need feed or supplies, I got work to do."

"No, you've been real helpful anyway." Daniel smiled a kind of secretive smile and turned to Mac. "Let's go."

When they passed through the exit, Mac glanced back.

"Is Hank still standing there?" Daniel asked without turning.

"No, he's headed toward Art's office." The same internal gut-level response knocked at

Mac's belly that struck immediately prior to the roadside bomb detonation in Iraq.

"That makes two members of the cult." Daniel stepped out into the gravel parking lot.

"And Toby makes three."

"That would be my take on it." Daniel slid his straw cowboy hat onto his head. "Guess we might want to pull a late night and find out what they're up to."

"I'm with you," Mac said. "I never suspected any-thing going on. Why now?"

"Bad times have funny ways of making people act different. Maybe we shouldn't play in this sandbox, Mac."

"Too late. I've already got a stake in this game they're playing."

"What, the goat we lost?"

Mac frowned. He hadn't considered the goat. One red-haired lady and her son had been at the top of his list of concerns. But his foreman didn't need to know that. "That's right. Someone, or something, killed my prize breeder."

A truck rumbled over the ruts in the parking lot and parked next to where Daniel and Mac stood.

"Here's our chance to question Cynthia's father on his lack of parenting." Mac nodded at the man inside the truck.

Jess Harding climbed down and tipped his hat. "Howdy, men. What brings you out and about?"

"Actually, I was looking for Toby Rice," Daniel stated.

The smile left Jess's face. "You won't find him here."

"Would we find him with your daughter?" Mac asked.

"Might be."

Daniel shook his head. "Why do you let Cynthia go out with that boy, Jess?"

"Nothing wrong with Toby." Jess jammed his hands into his front pockets. "His family's been here since this town was originally settled."

"And that makes beating up on your daughter okay?" Mac couldn't believe this man. He had a daughter to protect!

"He didn't mean to hurt her." Jess frowned and stared down at his boots. "Besides, it's really none of your business."

Mac glared at the man. "Someone needs to make it their business since you obviously aren't. She should press charges against Toby for assault and battery."

"She ain't gonna do that, so you can just stay out of it." Jess turned to go inside.

"So, Jess, are you involved with the cult as

well? Is that why you won't do anything about Toby?" Mac asked.

Jess froze in midstride.

Mac held his breath, hoping his comment broke through the silent treatment. He was destined to be disappointed when Art Nantan chose that moment to step through the door.

"Daniel, Mac, nice of you two to stop by. What can I do for you?"

"Answer some questions," Mac said, without holding anything back.

Art spread his arms wide. "Anything. Just ask."

"Where's Toby Rice?"

"Don't know. I fired him."

"What was it you were arguing about last night that brought you to blows?"

"As you may have noticed, Toby has a problem with authority figures. I called him on the carpet for being disrespectful." Art shrugged. "He didn't take it well. Why? Is he in some kind of trouble?"

Mac had to admit Art's story was probable.

"Maybe." Mac refrained from sharing that piece of information. "I just had some questions about the cult he might be involved in."

"I'm sorry. I don't know what you're talking about."

"There's been evidence of cult activities discovered down by the river. You telling me you don't know anything about it?"

"Sorry, I sure don't." Art smiled, a brief stretch of his lips. "Look, Mac, I have a business to run. I don't have time to play games with the locals. Besides, I'd be crazy to scare off my customers."

"Well, if you hear of any cult activities—"

"You'll be the first one I come to." Art nodded and smiled again.

"Howdy, neighbors!" Mayor Logan stepped across the street and into the parking lot. "Saw a group gathering and wondered what was going on."

Mac's muscles stiffened.

"Nothing," Art said.

Daniel stared hard at Art, and then turned to face the mayor. "That's right. Nothing's going on around here. At least that's what Art, Hank and Jess have to say. Guess I'll go back to the ranch and put my feet up."

"That's what I like about this town." Mayor Logan's grin broadened. "The slow, lazy pace. A great place to raise a family. Huh, Mac?"

Mac snorted and climbed into the passenger's seat of his truck. "Come on, Daniel. We have supplies to get."

Daniel climbed in behind the wheel and

shifted the truck into Reverse. "So, you think Toby's trying to scare Ms. Baxter?"

"Could be." Mac tapped his fingers on the armrest. "Thing about Toby is that he's a bully, more likely to use his brawn than his brain. I can believe he placed the lamb on her doorstep and even the snake. He could also be the one shooting at us. But I can't imagine him being clever enough to kill the larger livestock and making it look like an animal attack."

"Maybe someone else in the cult." Daniel shook his head. "I should stick to the ranch. At least there, I only have to work with dumb animals. Tell you the truth, Mac, these guys give me the creeps. And I used to consider them my friends."

"It's bad enough they're killing animals." Mac shook his head and stared out his window. "Let's hope they don't turn on the humans."

"Not a good time to be away from town, is it?" Dan paused before pulling out on the main highway. "You still up to running to Johnson City for those fencing supplies? I could pick them up by myself, if you want."

Mac inhaled and let out his breath in a long, steady stream. He was tempted to stay, his instincts telling him to stay close to Spirit Canyon, close to Eve and Joey, two people he had no hold on, no right to be concerned over. "No, we should be back well before dark. I don't think anything will happen during the daylight hours." But that didn't stop him from worrying.

THE EVENING CRAWLED by with the slow transition from gray day to black night. Eve paced the floor, the uneasy sense of impending doom weighing heavily on her chest, making it more difficult to breathe by the minute.

In his freshly painted room, Joey was fast asleep, completely worn-out from the excitement of finding a snake and playing at the store all afternoon.

Despite fatigue, Eve remained unsettled. She couldn't get Cynthia out of her head. Finally she grabbed the phone book and dialed Jess Harding's number.

Cynthia answered on the third ring. "Hello?"

"Oh, thank God it's you, Cynthia." Eve practically collapsed against the kitchen counter. "I was afraid you'd gone out." With Toby. She almost said it, but didn't.

"I was," she said. "I am."

"Cynthia!" Eve stopped and drew in a deep breath to calm herself. "Look, sweetie, if you're afraid of him, you can come stay with me. You don't have to go out with him."

"You shouldn't have called. It's not safe."

"Don't go, Cynthia. Come over to my house. Stay with me."

"He's waiting. I have to go." The line clicked dead.

She stood for a moment with the cordless phone still held to her ear. What now? How could she help someone who didn't want her interference? Chasing after the teenager wasn't an option with Joey sleeping soundly upstairs. And did she have any real evidence Cynthia was in mortal danger, besides the obvious bruises on her face?

No.

Eve dragged herself up the stairs to bed, knowing sleep would be, at worst, impossible, at best, fitful.

She lay down and closed her eyes, too exhausted to stay awake, yet afraid to go to sleep, dreading the dreams she knew would come.

THEY'D MADE the fencing supply store in Johnson City just before closing time and loaded up two rolls of fence and a couple boxes of nails.

Afterward, Mac drove over to the county

sheriff. He hadn't heard of any cult activity in their area, but he'd keep them informed if he did.

On the way back, Mac's gut knotted. They still had nothing to go on. Nothing.

Daniel shifted the truck into high. "Can't believe all this has been going on right under my nose all these years and I haven't heard a thing." He shook his head.

"Me, either."

"You got an excuse. You haven't been here."

Mac wondered if he had been here, could he have made a difference?

"Question is, how can we expose this cult and bring it to a halt?"

"And soon. I'm afraid someone's going to get hurt before we're all said and done." Mac hoped it wouldn't be Eve and Joey.

"Hank sure looked spooked when we talked to him," Daniel said, turning off the state highway onto the county road leading toward Spirit Canyon. Dusk had come early with the perpetual cloud cover. It would be after dark before they reached town.

"We'd do well to keep an eye open for that bunch from the feed store. Knowing we're on to them might make them try something."

Daniel reached over and flipped on the headlights. As his looked up, he glanced in the rearview mirror. His eyes widened. "Holy— Brace yourself!"

A loud bang exploded in Mac's ears and the truck slammed forward. Daniel jerked the steering wheel to keep the vehicle from sliding off the road into the ditch. He swerved, shooting gravel from the shoulders into the wheel wells.

Mac turned to see a set of headlights filling his vision, blindingly bright and bearing down on them again. The truck lurched forward, throwing Mac hard against his seat belt.

Daniel's head hit the steering wheel and he slumped in his seat.

Fighting his seat belt, Mac grabbed for the steering wheel, trying to maneuver the truck away from the ditch. But another bone-crunching impact sent them flying over the shoulder of the road and down into a ravine.

The truck bounced and careened forward. Mac could do nothing to slow their progress. Daniel was out cold with his foot on the accelerator. All Mac could do was hang on to the wheel and try to steer clear of any large objects like the sprawling oak tree looming out of the darkness.

Chapter Eleven

She couldn't see, but she knew they were just ahead. Clouds blocked the moon and stars from providing even the most remote light in the darkness.

As she trudged forward, she worried about Joey, home alone in his bed. Would he wake in the night and cry out for her? Would he be frightened when he found she was gone?

Although her instincts were to protect her son, she couldn't force her feet to move back toward her house. Predestined to approach the light, she took a deep breath and brushed the bristly branches of scrub cedar aside and peered through to a clearing.

As in her last dream, a ring of fire blazed in the center of a circle of men all dressed in hooded capes. The only difference was this time a girl stood among them.

Cynthia.

Eve gasped, the sound drowned out by the chanting.

The same man stepped into the circle carrying a small animal—a pure white goat kid. As he held it high above his head, the chanting ceased, to be replaced by the frightened cries of the kid.

Cynthia stared at the goat, as if in a trance, her face pale, her eyes glazed.

Eve blinked and the man held a shiny chalice aloft where, only a moment ago, he'd held the goat. "Hail, devourer of blood, who camest forth from the block of slaughter."

The ring of men shouted, "Hail!"

"Hail to the spirit of the wolf, may he lead us out of the darkness of despair. Let him lead us to greatness!"

"Hail!"

"Now drink the blood of innocence. Drink to our new sister!" The leader lifted the goblet to his lips and drank. Then he passed through the fire and handed it to Cynthia.

She stared down at the chalice in the man's hand.

"Don't do it," Eve whispered.

Cynthia shoved the chalice, and blood spilled over the leader's cloak. "No!"

"That's my girl. Don't do it," Eve urged from her hiding place behind the brush.

One of the hooded men moved up behind the girl, blocking any chance of escape.

Eve tried to rise, but her legs wouldn't work. When she opened her mouth to scream, her voice was silent.

As if sensing her there, the hooded man behind Cynthia stared straight at Eve, his eyes reflecting the red and orange glow of the flames.

Eve watched in frozen horror as the hooded one with the red eyes grabbed Cynthia's hair and jerked her head back. "Drink to strength, that those who would keep you down will fall before you." He poured the liquid down Cynthia's throat. Then he shoved her aside and raised the chalice high. As he did, he stepped into the circle of fire.

"Are you all sheep that you would allow others to prosper while your pockets are empty? Would you lose your homes and your heritage while others reap the benefits of the land?"

"No!" the group shouted.

The sound reverberated in Eve's chest and ears. She was sure she'd recognized some of the voices of the men shouting, yet their faces remained shadowed, dark like the starless night.

"Then don't stand by while they rape the land and profit, while you toil, yet still lose your heritage. Go forth and take back what was once yours."

The red-eyed man shouted, "Hail to the leader!"

"Hail!"

"There are those asking questions about the cult of the wolf." The red-eyed one called out in a strong, clear voice. "There are those who would disband our brothers and sister.

"Let no man tear us asunder." Red eyes gleamed maniacally from beneath the dark hood, but his voice remained calm, resonant and compelling in its evil. "The pack is family. Only here can you find solace. Only within the pack will you find peace. Through our combined strength we become whole again. Deal with those who would harm the pack of the wolf."

The original leader stepped in beside the red-eyed man. "Wait, how do you mean?"

"With whatever means necessary."

"You mean kill someone?"

Eve's breath caught in her throat and she didn't dare stir. She had to know the red-eyed demon's answer.

"If the need calls for it." His head tipped forward and the red eyes narrowed.

Eve shivered and squirmed as if she were on the receiving end of that deadly stare.

"We don't kill people," the leader said.

"Getting squeamish? Were you not the one

who started this group because of the injustices reaped upon you and its members? Do you retain the strength to lead these men through hard times?"

"Yes, but we've never killed anyone."

"If you cannot lead the pack, step down," the red-eyed one said.

"You can't make me do that. I started this pack thirty years ago. It's mine."

"You are superfluous and unworthy of your following," the red-eyed man towered over the old leader, pressing closer.

"Like hell I am. These are my people." The other man spoke strong words, but his voice shook. He took one step backward, then another, until he stood with his back almost touching the fire.

"They were your people. But now it is time for you to step aside."

"I won't!"

"You will," the man with the red eyes said in a whisper.

Eve could hear what he said even from across the field, and her blood froze in her veins. The threat in those words was enough for her to run screaming, if she could move.

The original leader snorted and shoved the red-eyed man aside. Then he stepped toward the circle of men and raised his arms, "Hail to the pack! Hail to the powerful spirit of the wolf!"

"Hail!" The cries rose above the treetops, to be absorbed into the hovering clouds.

As the scary man with the blood-red eyes eased out of the ring of fire, the leader waved his hand. "Bring the girl forward," he commanded.

Cynthia was shoved into the circle of fire. Her face was a mask of revulsion and fear, blood drying on her chin.

"You are one of the pack. You will always be one of the pack as long as you live. What you see and hear stays within the family. Do you understand?"

Eve knew that meant the teenager couldn't get out of it now that she was in.

Cynthia nodded, her eyes round as saucers.

"That goes for the entire pack," the leader told the men around the circle. "Hail to the pack!"

"Hail!"

Her stomach twisting, Eve pressed a hand to her mouth. Oh God, what had Cynthia gotten herself into? No wonder she was so scared.

A RINGING SOUND jerked Eve back.

Back from the fire. Back from the woods. Back to her house, her room, her bed.

She opened her eyes and stared at the ceiling.

The ringing continued. It was the phone on the nightstand. For a full five seconds, Eve couldn't move. The sheer terror of her dream froze her body in place.

When her heart started beating again, she sat up and grabbed the telephone. "Hello?"

She held her breath again, expecting a continuation of the voices in her dream.

"Eve? This is Addie."

Light-headed from lack of oxygen, Eve sank back against the pillows and inhaled deeply. With her relief so complete, all she could choke past her vocal chords was a gravelly, "Hi."

"I'm sorry. Did I wake you up?"

"Yes, but I'm glad you did."

"Are you okay?" Addie's voice sounded worried, concerned.

Other than having a dream from hell, Eve was all right. "Yes, I'm fine." She glanced at the clock on the table beside her. Two o'clock? "Good Lord, look at the time. Addie, is something wrong?"

"Yeah." She heaved a long sigh, her breath blowing static in the phone. "There's been an accident."

Instantly flashbacks assaulted Eve. The police at her door, telling her these same words. She leaped from the bed, the cordless phone in her hand, and ran for Joey's room. It took only seconds to confirm her son slept on, his angelic face at peace. Though Eve knew Joey wasn't the one, she couldn't have stopped her mad rush if she'd wanted to. The accident had happened to someone else and Addie was still on the phone. Afraid to ask, but afraid not to, she did. "Who?"

"Daniel and Mac."

EVE HURRIED ALONG the Emergency Room corridor at University Hospital in Johnson City. She kept reminding herself to breathe. Mac might need her and she couldn't risk passing out without knowing how he was.

Addie stopped in front of the information window. "Can you tell me where I can find Mac McGuire and Daniel Goodman?"

Without glancing up, the woman behind the glass clicked away at the keyboard. Finally, she looked up. "I show Daniel Goodman in room 214. I don't have a Mac McGuire listed."

Eve's heart stuttered in her chest. Where was Mac? She leaned toward the window, her hands gripping the counter. "Would they have taken him to a different hospital?"

"I don't know. Sometimes the different ambulance services deliver to other hospitals in the area. If you wait a moment, I can check."

Addie stepped back and took a good look at Eve. Her lips tightened and she hooked her arm through Eve's. "Come with me." She led her to the cushioned seating in the waiting area. "Sit before you fall."

"But we have to find Mac."

"Look, I'll go ask. But in the meantime, I can't be worrying about you passing out on the floor next to me. Take a deep breath."

Eve sucked in a lungful of air and blew it out. "There. I'm fine." She leaned forward to stand, but Addie's hand stayed her.

"Eve, he'll be just fine." Addie smiled. "This isn't your ex-husband. Mac is as tough as they come. He'll be all right."

"I can't help it. Last time I was in a hospital…"

"I know. Now, don't you worry. I'll be right back."

Eve leaned back in the chair and closed her eyes, concentrating on pushing back the monstrous panic attack threatening to overwhelm her. Images of Joey lying in a hospital bed with his head bandaged, his eyes staring straight ahead in a trance, flooded her memory. Visions of her ex-husband lying in the morgue, his face and arms ravaged by dog bites, swam in her memory. The thought of seeing Mac dead or dying was killing her. Mac had come into her and Joey's life when they'd needed him most. He was strong and caring…and she might just be falling in love with him.

"Is this seat taken?"

At the sound of the deep, resonant voice, Eve's eyes popped open. "Mac!" She leaped from her seat and flung her arms around his neck. "You're alive. You're okay."

"Yes, I am." His arms came up around her and held her close. "I tried to call your house, but you'd already left."

Eve pressed her face into his chest, fighting but losing the battle to keep the tears from falling. "I thought…"

"It's okay."

"But I thought you were dead," she sobbed.

He chuckled, his breath stirring her hair. "Can't get rid of me that easily."

When Eve's heart slowed and her tears dried, she realized what a scene she must be making and pushed away.

But Mac kept her within the circle of his arms and stared down at her. "You were really worried, weren't you?"

"Yes, of course." She brushed the back of her hand over her eyes, her cheeks flooding with warmth. "Anyone would be worried about a friend being in an accident. How's Daniel?"

"Surviving just fine." Mac's knuckles brushed against her cheekbone as he pushed a strand of her hair behind her cheek. "Are *you* okay?"

With a shaky laugh, Eve glanced down at where her hands rested against Mac's chest. "I'm not the one who's been in a car wreck." She let her gaze study his face for any signs of injury. "You weren't hurt?"

"No. Now, stop worrying and no more crying." He pressed a kiss to the end of her nose. "It makes your nose red."

Heat rose again in her cheeks and she lifted fingers to her nose. "Is it that bad?"

He shook his head and kissed her nose again. "No. Red looks good on you."

With each touch of his lips, Eve's stomach flip-flopped. The thought of losing Mac had nearly had her swooning. But the reality of being in his strong arms was making her increasingly dizzy.

Addie chose that moment to join Mac and Eve. "The nurse said he's got a bump on his head and they'll keep him for overnight observation, but he should be just fine."

Eve's face burned hotter and she stepped out of Mac's arms. "I'm glad he's going to be okay."

"Daniel's as hardheaded as they come. He'll be back swearing at goats by tomorrow afternoon."

Mac pushed a hand through his hair and sighed. "I'm beat. Could you two give me a lift home?"

"Sure," Addie said. "Long as you fill us in on what happened."

"Deal."

Mac insisted on driving Eve's SUV, for which Eve was eternally grateful. Her hands were still shaking and she wasn't sure she could concentrate with Mac in such close quarters.

"So, spill, already." Addie said from the back seat as soon as the car doors closed.

"Not much to tell," Mac hedged. "First, tell me, where's Joey?"

"I left him with Laura Taylor," Eve replied. "He'll be thrilled to play with Katie when he wakes up."

"Good."

"Don't make me crawl across the back of this seat to hurt you, young man. What in tarnation happened?" Addie's voice held no patience.

"Someone ran us off the road on the way back from Johnson City."

"What?" Eve's heart leaped into her throat. "Who?"

"Unfortunately it happened in the dark, whoever it was had their brights on. The glare blinded us. We never saw the vehicle, but the lights were high off the ground, like a truck."

"Oh, God," Eve pressed a hand to her chest.

"Ran right into you?" Addie wondered out loud. "What kind of fool drives like that?"

"Someone who wants to see us in a ditch." In the glow from the dash, Mac's fingers were white as they gripped the wheel.

"You think they did it on purpose?" Addie asked.

"Yeah."

"Why?" Eve asked.

"All I could figure was that we asked too many questions this afternoon."

"What do you mean?"

"I went fishing at the feed store and opened a can of worms." Their questions had almost gotten them killed. He wished he'd at least gotten a look at the truck that rammed them.

"You sure you didn't get conked on the head, too, Mac?" Addie said. "You aren't makin' much sense."

"Not much of anything has been making sense lately," Eve added.

"You're telling me." He reached across and curled his fingers around Eve's. Her reaction to seeing him in the hospital was on instant replay in his mind. She tugged a little on her hand but he wasn't letting go. Her skin was silky smooth and cool to the touch, but felt good wrapped in his.

Eventually she gave up trying to free her hand back, and she returned the pressure. "What kind of questions were you asking that inspired such a response?"

"Questions about Toby Rice and the cult we've been hearing rumors about."

Eve gasped and her hand that had been cool before seemed to go even colder beneath his.

"What?" Mac shot a glance at Eve. "Have you heard something?"

"As a matter of fact, we did earlier this afternoon." Addie sat forward. "Bernie Odom was just a fount of information. Seems they invited him to join back when his ranch was in trouble. He declined. And they haven't asked him since. Appears the cult developed out of a group of ranchers who were down on their luck, back in that really bad dry spell we had thirty years ago. It's been going on since then. Bernie thinks it flares up every time there's some serious bad luck."

"So, it's not just the teens, then." Mac stared straight ahead, his hand tightening around Eve's. "Well, their luck is about to get worse."

Mac dropped Addie at the General Store, and for the rest of the journey to his ranch, Eve sat in silence.

Was she regretting their intimacy at the hospital? Mac held tight to her hand, refusing to give up on her. After his brush with death, he realized the overwhelming need for the warmth of a woman's hand. And the need was growing into all-out hunger. More than the touch of her fingers in his, he wanted to pull her into his arms and hold her close, never letting go.

In a few short minutes, he pulled Eve's SUV into his driveway and slowed to a stop. Reluctantly he let go of her hand and slid from her vehicle to the ground, circling around to open her door for her.

But Eve had already climbed down and closed the door. For a few uncomfortable moments she stood there, scuffing the toe of her shoe in the gravel.

This was the part where she'd remind him she didn't want a relationship. His chest tightened and he braced himself for her words.

After a painfully long silence, she looked up into his face, the glow of the headlights highlighting the deep auburn of her hair. "I'm glad you didn't get hurt."

Mac let the air he'd been holding out of his lungs in a sigh, then tugged Eve into his arms. "I'm glad you're glad," he whispered against her hair. Then he tipped her head back and claimed her lips with all the hunger and desire he'd stockpiled since he'd first met this remarkable woman. He kissed her as if there was no tomorrow, and with Eve and her adamance about stepfathers, there might not be a tomorrow for them.

But the astonishing fact was that she was kissing him back. Her slim, graceful hands slid inside his shirt and tangled in the hairs covering his chest.

Trying not to scare her away, he pressed her closer, the evidence of his desire a hard ridge pressing into her belly. He wanted her more than he'd wanted anything or anyone in his life. He loved her fierceness and bravery concerning her son. He admired her determination to make a home for her and Joey in Spirit Canyon. Despite her slender build and delicate features, she was strong and capable, a woman a man could sink into and love for the rest of his life.

Too soon, she pushed away from him, her breathing sounding like a marathon runner after the push to the finish line. Her chest rose and fell in heaving gusts. "We shouldn't...I need... Ah, hell." She leaned her head against his chest and groaned. "I have to go."

"You could stay," he suggested.

"No." With a sigh, she turned away from him. "I can't. I have to get back."

Mac could have kicked himself. He'd pressured her too soon, instead of giving her time to come to grips with what was building between them. Because something was definitely happening, and he didn't want it to end.

With a deep breath and an attempt at bringing himself under control, Mac forced words past his tight lips. "Are you sure you don't want to stay the night with Addie?"

"No. I'll be fine by myself. I'd better get going." She turned back to him, her face beautiful in the light from the SUV, her lips swollen from his kisses.

God, how he wanted her. But Mac held himself in check, nodding instead of grabbing her back into his arms. "Be careful and call me when you get there."

"I will. And Mac?"

He pressed a finger to her lips to keep her from saying their kiss was a mistake. "I'll see you tomorrow."

With a weak smile, she nodded and climbed into her vehicle. Within seconds, her taillights disappeared down his driveway and Mac was alone.

Exhausted, bruised and disheartened by the

day's events, Mac entered the empty ranch house. The only light in the darkness was Eve and their incredible kiss.

How could all this drama with dead animals, live snakes and cult activities be happening? Had everyone in Spirit Canyon gone crazy? He didn't know whom to trust anymore.

With an angry flick of his wrist he tossed his hat on the kitchen table, dragged out the can of coffee grounds and measured a heaping spoonful into the coffeemaker. At four o'clock in the morning, he knew we wouldn't be able to go back to sleep. He might as well start the day.

After a quick shower, he checked his answering machine. Eve had left a brief message saying she'd made it to Addie's. Well, what did he expect? A declaration of undying love?

The smell of fresh-brewed coffee drew Mac back into the kitchen. He was pouring a cup and watching the sun rise up beneath the layer of ever-present clouds when the telephone rang.

Dread slowed the blood in his veins. What could have happened now? As he reached for the phone, thoughts of Dan in the hospital flitted across his mind, followed by Eve. Did she make it to Addie's all right? He should have called. No. He should never have let her go alone.

Mac jerked the phone off the charger and barked, "Yes?"

"Mac, this is Sheriff Hodges. I thought you should know, we found Art Nantan's body in the river just a few minutes ago."

Chapter Twelve

Mac had never felt more mentally or emotionally exhausted in all his life than when he stepped through the door of the General Store after noon.

Eve was leaning against the back counter next to Addie and Laura when Sheriff Hodges and Mac walked in. Although Addie had opened the store later than usual, apparently the news had spread quickly.

"You've heard?" the sheriff asked.

The three women nodded.

Eve moved toward Mac and rested her hand on his arm. "How's Daniel?"

"He'll live." He wanted to pull her into his arms and hug her close. But not now. Not in front of everyone. Instead he stared down at her fingers, then up into her eyes, wanting to say so much more than he dared. So he kept his scrambled thoughts to himself.

"You look beat," she said.

And he felt beat. In more ways than one.

Sheriff Hodges didn't look much better. "Got the state crime lab working on the murder scene now. Not much a small town sheriff can do at this point but get in the way. I did order a scan of the crime database to see if there was a match on this particular type of attack." The sheriff sat on a stool and set his cowboy hat on the counter. "I don't suppose you have a cup of coffee behind that counter, do you, Ms. Addie?"

"As a matter of fact, I just made a fresh pot. Let me get you some." Addie hurried toward a shiny new coffee urn on a shelf against the back wall.

"What happened?" Eve asked, a concerned frown marring her beautiful face. She didn't need all this worry, didn't deserve it. Hadn't she already had enough hardship in her life?

Mac wanted to ease her burden, but he couldn't. He didn't know who'd killed Art or where the killer would strike next. "Looked like the same attacker that got my breeder goat and Dottie Baumgartner's miniature stallion."

"Animal attack?" Eve's gaze met his. "So it wasn't the hogs. Do you think it was a wolf?" Her question was directed at him in a little above a whisper.

"I don't know what to think anymore." Mac scrubbed a hand through his hair and sank onto a stool.

Eve sat next to him, her gaze panning the store for Joey. The child was playing quietly with Katie, stacking soup cans from one of the grocery shelves.

Laura leaned her elbows on the counter. "I thought the scare was about that cult thing going on. How can an entire town not know about something like that happening in their midst?" She shook her head. "It's times like these I'm glad my husband snores. At least I know where he is at night. Too many strange things happening in the wee hours lately."

"Sheriff, have you seen Cynthia since last night?" Eve asked.

"No." Sheriff Hodges brushed his hand against his pant leg. "But I'd like to get hold of her boyfriend for some questioning. Right now Toby's the only one I know with a reason to kill Art."

Mac's head came up. "Are you talking about the fight before the hog hunt?"

"Yeah." He stared hard at Mac. "Do you remember anything else they said to each other?"

"Something about Art's time being up." Mac strained his tired brain to recall every detail.

"Art called him a punk kid who didn't know when to keep his mouth shut."

"With Toby's temper that may have been enough." The sheriff shook his head. "Need to find that boy. Got an APB out on him with the state."

"Toby's not the only one with a grudge against Art Nantan," Addie said. "There was a time half the ranchers in the county hated that man."

"How so?" The sheriff glanced at Addie, his head tipped to the side.

"He worked as the loan officer at the bank while he was getting his feed store up and running. Art managed the liens on almost all the ranches. Including yours, Mac."

"I didn't know that," Mac said. Neither his father nor Daniel had ever mentioned that little piece of news.

"When the drought hit thirty years ago, it wiped out quite a few ranches whose families had been working this county for the past hundred years. The bank made Art responsible for foreclosing on all the liens and a lot of ranchers lost everything. Although he managed to put a few of them to work in his feed store, many of the ranchers were forced to migrate to the cities." Addie rubbed her dust rag across the counter and then stared down, as if seeing the past, not the polished wood. "Not long afterward, Art lost his own ranch due to the drought. But he managed to keep his feed store afloat."

"You think someone out there is carrying a thirty-year-old grudge?" Laura asked. "It just doesn't make sense. Why would a killer wait so long to get even? It wasn't even his bank. He may not have had a choice."

Sheriff Hodges made notes on his pad. "Seems if Art's death had anything to do with the fact that he foreclosed on properties, the killer would have taken him down sooner."

"You're probably right." Addie tucked her dust rag in a pocket of her apron. "But old anger can run deep, especially when you've lost the only home you ever knew."

"Which ranchers did Art foreclose on?" the sheriff asked.

"There's Hank Bleumfeld, Jack Adams, Dathan Rice and Jess Harding, to name a few."

The sheriff tapped his pen on the notepad. "Most of them work at the feed store."

"That's right." Addie shrugged. "Like I said, the ones that stayed went to work for Art at the feed store."

"Interesting." Sheriff Hodges closed his notebook and tucked it in his shirt pocket. "Guess I better start there."

Laura shook her head. "If you're heading for the feed store, it's closed on account of the murder and investigation."

"Then I'll just have to hunt them down one by one." The lawman headed for the door.

"Sheriff," Mac called after him. "I'd like to go with you when you question Jess Harding. I want to check on Cynthia."

"I'll call you on your cell phone when I'm headed out that way. I better go now. I'm supposed to meet with the state police out at Art's place. Maybe we'll find some useful information in his house."

"Let us know whatever you can," Mac said.

"You bet. I don't care what the rule book says about confidentiality of a case. When people start dying, I'd rather everyone know too much than too little." The sheriff tipped his hat. "Y'all stay safe."

"You, too, Sheriff." As soon as Hodges left through the screen door, Mac turned back to Eve. "I don't have a good feeling about all this. I'm especially worried about you living on the edge of town all alone."

Eve's back straightened. "I'm not all alone. I have Joey."

"You know what I mean."

"You could move in with me, Eve," Addie

offered, "if you're afraid of going back to the house."

"I'm not afraid," she said. Her strong response didn't mean much to Mac when she bit down on her lip, frown lines appearing on her forehead.

"You know, Mac and Addie have a point," Laura jumped in.

"It's just you and a four-year-old boy. Did you do anything about buying a gun?" Mac asked.

Eve shook her head. "Not yet. I'm still not sure I'm comfortable with a gun in the house."

"Look at what's happened already. Full-grown animals have been killed. You've had a dead lamb and a live snake deposited at your house. Daniel and Mac were run off the road last night and a man is dead." Laura planted her fists on her hips. "I'd say there's a good chance you're on someone's list and it's getting short. You don't want to end up like Art, do you?"

"I refuse to be driven from my home." Eve's voice lacked some of her earlier conviction.

"There's stubborn and there's foolish." Laura wrapped an arm around Eve's shoulder. "At least let someone stay with you if you're not going to move in with Ms. Addie."

"I can manage on my own." She pushed her shoulders back and stepped away from Laura's touch. "But, Mac, I would like to keep Molly around. She's proven to be a good watchdog."

"I'll drop her off later." Mac looked across at her son. "Will Joey be all right with a dog around all the time?"

"I guess he'll have to be okay with Molly, considering she'll be our protection."

Mac scowled, but didn't push the issue. Eve could be stubborn and she wasn't ready for his help. "If you won't get a gun, at least take this." He unclipped his hunting knife from his belt. "It folds up small enough to put in your pocket. Carry it." Mac realized he was sounding bossy and softened his words with a lopsided smile. He lifted her hand and placed the knife in her palm, closing her fingers around the neatly folded blade.

Her green eyes stared back at him and the pulse in her neck was beating fast, but she kept the knife and nodded. "Okay."

"I'm going to pick up Daniel from the hospital, then I'll be out at the ranch tending livestock. If anyone needs me, I'll keep my cell phone handy."

Reluctant to go to her empty house, Eve hung around the store for another thirty minutes. As much as she wanted to prove her independence, she couldn't help the quiver of fear that shot across her nerves when she thought of sleeping there again.

Laura had stayed as well. "Do you think this town will ever be back to normal, Addie?"

"I don't think this town will ever be the same." Addie paused in midsweep with her broom. "But I do think it will be a good place to live again. Eventually. Let's just hope it's sooner than later."

The bell over the screen door rang and all three women turned. Eve half expected more bad news.

Cynthia Harding hurried in, her chin down, heading straight for the rows of over-the-counter medicines.

"Cynthia! Oh, thank God you're okay." Eve ran up to the girl and put her hand on her arm.

The teenager jerked back. "Don't touch me." Her sharp words were so uncharacteristic for Cynthia.

Hurt and a little frightened by her reaction, Eve stepped back. "I was worried about you."

"I don't need you to worry about me."

"We were all worried about you, Cynthia." Addie leaned her broom against the wall and stood next to Eve.

"Who asked for your concern, anyway?" Since she'd walked into the store, Cynthia hadn't lifted her head once. She stared stubbornly at the floor. "I just need something for a headache and I'll be out of here."

"But, Cynthia, you can't leave." Eve clasped her arm and held on when the girl tried to shake her off. "Bad things are happening lately. You're scared of the cult, aren't you?"

The teenager stared up into Eve's eyes. Her look of desolation and fear was so intense Eve fought the urge to drop her arm and reel backward.

"Leave me alone." All the anger had fled Cynthia's voice. Her words came out in a whispered plea. "I don't need your help or anyone else's. It's too late."

"Cynthia, it's never too late." Addie stepped forward and slid her arm around the girl. "We can get the sheriff to help. The law will protect you."

For a moment she leaned into Addie's arms, her eyes glistening with unshed tears. Then her jaw tightened and she pushed away. "No! You can't help me. No one can."

She pressed her hands to her face and raced for the door.

Eve ran after her, catching her by the elbow on the sidewalk outside the store. She couldn't let Cynthia go, not after the dreams. "Don't run away. Let us help you."

Cynthia scanned the street, her eyes wide and

worried. "Don't talk to me. It'll only be trouble. Besides, no one can help me now."

"I know what you're up against." Eve drew in a deep breath, knowing what she was about to say would sound crazy. "I know about the cult. I saw what happened to you."

"What do you know? You weren't there."

"I saw it. The ring of fire, the men in capes."

Cynthia's eyes widened and her breathing grew shallow. "How could you?"

"I saw it in my dream." Eve held the girl's hands in hers. "I know what they made you drink." A chill slithered across her skin and her stomach lurched at the vision conjured in her memory.

"How?" Tears welled in Cynthia's eyes and she shook her head. "It doesn't matter how. You can't tell anyone or your life will be in danger. I have to go. They can't see me talking to you."

"Call me. We can work this out."

"No, we can't." She peeled Eve's fingers from her arm.

At that moment Mayor Logan stepped out of his office a few doors down, smiled and waved. "Hello, Eve, Cynthia."

Cynthia's face paled even more. She turned toward Eve and whispered, "It's too late." Then she turned and ran down the street.

Eve didn't try to stop her this time. All the girl's fear and desperation hit her squarely in the gut. She'd experienced it in her dream last night and knew the hopelessness Cynthia felt.

"Cynthia sure was in a hurry." The mayor strode down the sidewalk toward Eve, a frown denting his smooth forehead. "Was it something I said?"

"No. Not at all. Excuse me." Eve returned to the store and Joey.

AFTER MAC DROPPED Daniel at the house with strict instructions to take it easy, he got a call from the sheriff to meet him out at Jess Harding's place. They agreed to meet at the highway turnoff. Mac followed Sheriff Hodges down the country road that led to what was left of Jess Harding's homestead, a run-down house on two acres.

The sheriff climbed down from his SUV and met Mac at his truck. "Found some interesting items at Art's place."

"Let me guess." Mac's eyes narrowed. "Cult paraphernalia?"

"You got it. Everything from fancy carved-handled knives to a hooded, black cape. It's stuff right out of a horror movie, if you ask me."

"And if Art is involved in the cult, I'd bet

my ranch a lot of the men working for him are also involved."

Sheriff Hodges adjusted his shoulder holster and nodded toward the Harding house. "Let's find out."

The sheriff knocked on the door. They waited a minute and he knocked again. Still, no answer. On the third knock, Jess Harding jerked the door open and shouted, "What?" He stood in a worn pair of pajama bottoms and a stained V-neck undershirt.

"Good afternoon, Jess." Sheriff Hodges's eyebrows rose as he greeted the man.

"Oh, Sheriff, it's you." Jess ran his hand through his bed hair and scratched at his chest. "What can I do for you?"

Mac shifted, drawing Jess's attention to himself.

The older man's eyes narrowed slightly.

"Are you aware Art Nantan was found facedown in the river this morning?"

"What?" Jess's face bleached white and he staggered back a step. "Art? Art Nantan? Dead?"

His stunned reaction was too genuine for Jess Harding to be the killer. Mac immediately scratched him off his list of suspects.

"I have a few questions I'd like to ask you," the sheriff said.

"Am I a suspect?" If Jess's face could get any whiter, he'd be a dead man.

"No, not unless you want to confess to a killing." Sheriff Hodges pulled out his trusty notebook and pen. "When was the last time you saw Art Nantan?"

Jess's gaze darted from the sheriff to Mac and back to the sheriff. "Uh, at the feed store yesterday at quitting time."

"Did you see him later that evening?"

Jess's gaze didn't meet Sheriff Hodges's or Mac's. "No. I said I saw him last at the feed store at quittin' time. Unless you plan on arresting me or takin' me in for questionin', I've said all I've got to say."

"I'm not done yet." Sheriff Hodges's mouth tightened. "Are you a member of a local cult?"

"No," he answered a little too quickly. "I don't know nothin' about no cult."

The sheriff pressed on and hit him with his next question. "Do you know whether or not Art Nantan was a member of the local cult?"

"I told you, I don't know nothin' about no cult." Jess shot a glaring look at Mac. "Whatcha starin' at?"

"You, I suppose." Mac's lips tightened. "For someone who doesn't know anything, you're sure jumpy."

"What's it to you, anyway? You ain't part of the law." Jess turned to the sheriff. "Why's he here?"

Without looking up from the notes he was making in his notebook, the sheriff answered, "He came along as a concerned citizen."

"That's right." Mac stepped forward. "I'm worried about your daughter."

"She ain't none of your concern."

"Do you know where she is?" Mac asked.

"Nope. Ain't seen her since last night."

"As a father, that doesn't alarm you?"

"She's a big girl." Jess glared at Mac. "Besides it's none of your business."

Mac's fists clenched. He wanted to hit this man for his indifference to his daughter. "Someone needs to make her their business."

"And who asked you?" Jess puffed out his chest and stepped across the threshold. "Look, I may not have a big fancy ranch like you, but you got no right to come on my property and ask questions. As far as I'm concerned, you're trespassin'."

Sheriff Hodges stepped between the two men. "Come on, Mac. I've asked all the questions I needed." He turned toward Jess. "I suggest you find your daughter and don't be goin' anywhere. The state police may want to come by and question you later."

"Let 'em. I ain't got nothin' to hide." With

that parting comment, Jess Harding walked back into the house and slammed the door.

"Oh, I bet you don't have anything to hide," the sheriff muttered loud enough only Mac could hear him.

When Mac reached the sheriff's SUV, he stood with his back to the house. "My gut feeling is Jess didn't know Art had been killed."

"Right. And he looked kinda green around the gills about it." The lawman removed his hat and shoved a hand through his hair. "But he sure as hell was hiding a boat load of information about that cult. Wouldn't look at me while he was answering my questions."

"Think you could get a warrant to search Harding's house for a link to the cult activities?"

"I'll put a call in to the district judge as soon as I get back to the office."

"And, Sheriff, if you see Cynthia, let me know."

"Yeah. With Toby out of pocket, I'm worried about her myself."

Mac jammed his Stetson on his head and climbed into his truck.

With all the talk about cults and one man dead, he was feeling pretty uneasy about Eve and Joey living on the edge of town. He was due to deliver Molly there, but was Molly enough? He'd like to leave more than a dog at Eve's house. He'd like to stay there himself. Molly was loyal and protective, but if Art's killer, whether man or beast, was big enough to take out a full grown man and a miniature horse, who was to say he couldn't take out a small woman and her child?

Mac sighed. He had a dog to deliver to Eve's house. And the sooner the better.

Chapter Thirteen

Eve picked up a paintbrush and swiped a few strokes across the wall in the living room before she turned back to the window. Why couldn't she focus on her task? She had the entire living room to paint today and she hadn't even covered half of one wall in the past two hours. Joey had completed the lower half of a four-foot section before he grew bored and dug out his Tonka trucks to play with on the kitchen floor.

Eve was watching for Mac and Molly. She couldn't wait for the dog to be in place, guarding her house. If she was honest, she wasn't as anxious to see the dog as to see its owner. She felt safe when Mac was around. As much as she wanted to be free and independent, she allowed her guard to relax when he was near. And she wanted to discuss what had occurred at the store after he'd left.

After her tenth pass from the wall to the

windows, she covered the paint can and carried her brush to the sink in the kitchen. Who was she fooling, anyway? She couldn't paint with all that was going on with Art's death and Cynthia's flight from the store. A cup of tea might at least calm her.

As she set a kettle on the burner, she heard the rumble of an engine in the driveway. Her heartbeat hopped into high gear and she raced for the window.

Relief mixed with anticipation when she recognized the vehicle as Mac's. Feathering her fingers through her hair, she was stepping toward the door when the phone rang.

Drat! With a quick glance toward the truck, Eve turned for the telephone in the hallway and lifted it from the receiver. "Hello?"

"Eve!" Cynthia's voice crackled over the line. "I n— your help."

"Cynthia, you're breaking up." Eve pressed the receiver to her ear in hopes she could hear more clearly.

"I'm on —ll phone. —fraid to g—ome."

"Come to my house, Cynthia. Let me help you."

"Can't. —s not safe."

"Who's trying to hurt you?"

"T— later—"

For a moment Eve thought the cell phone cut out completely and she strained desperately to hear Cynthia's next words.

"Cynthia, let me meet you somewhere. I can help. Please let me help."

"Eve? What's wrong?" a voice called out behind her.

Eve spun toward Mac as he burst through the screen door.

"It's Cynthia. She's scared."

He grabbed the phone with one hand and wrapped his other arm around her shoulders. "Cynthia, this is Mac. Where are you?"

Eve leaned into his warmth and strength, inhaling the purely male scent of Mac. For a moment she closed her eyes and willed everything to be right with her world.

"Let us help you, Cynthia. If we can't meet you where you are now, tell us where we can." He held his breath and pressed the phone harder to his ear. "I didn't get that. Say again?"

On her tiptoes, Eve pressed her ear to the back of the phone, straining to hear what Cynthia was saying.

"The cave with the Native pictures by the river?" His arm tightened around Eve's shoulders. "Keep safe, Cynthia. We'll meet you there in two hours. What's that?" He listened for a moment then stared at the phone and pressed it back to his ear. "Got cut off."

"What did she say?" Eve clutched at Mac's shirt and stared up at him. "Are we going to meet her? Where?"

"You're right. She's terrified. She's trying to stay clear of town. And, Eve, she said she knows who killed Art."

"Ah, jeez." She leaned her forehead against his chest. "If that person has any idea that she knows, he'll be after her. Oh God. Poor Cynthia. What are we going to do?"

Mac laid the phone in its cradle and pulled her into both arms. "We have to wait and meet her in two hours at the caves along the riverbank."

"Where's that?"

"I'll take you there. For now, let's find someone to watch Joey for a couple hours."

"Mac?" Eve wrapped her arms around his waist and buried her face against his chest. "I'm scared."

He pressed his lips to her hair. "You should stay in town with Joey."

"No. Cynthia called me to help. I can't stay here not knowing."

"Then let's get Joey someplace safe. And, if we don't want anyone following us, we should go in on horses."

"Horses?"

"I didn't even think about it. Do you ride?"

She gave him a shaky smile. "I haven't in about ten years."

"You'll be okay. It's like falling off a bicycle. I'm afraid if I park a vehicle close to where we're going, whoever is after her might figure it out."

"You're right." She inhaled a deep breath and smiled. "Let's saddle up, cowboy."

MAC GLANCED BACK at Eve. She had a death grip on the saddle horn, but she was hanging in there. He'd given her the gentlest horse in his stable and she hadn't complained once on the long ride across his ranch to the river.

Twenty minutes after they'd left the barn, the wind had picked up, tossing the clouds into a frenzy, and streaks of lightning bolted across the sky. Mac already regretted suggesting they take the horses. In violent weather, even the most docile mount could become skittish. Yet, Eve insisted they press on.

With a firm hand on the reins, Mac held his gelding to the trail, nudging him forward. They were to meet Cynthia at the caves in less than five minutes and they still had a way to go.

As much as they needed the rain, Mac hoped it would hold off until all three of them were home safe. Riding out in the open in a lightning storm wasn't something he'd recommend, especially for inexperienced riders.

Another glance at Eve in the waning light only served to reinforce his original opinion. She should have stayed with Addie. Her face was pale and her hands gripped the reins and saddle horn so tightly, her fingers were white. Lines of worry etched a path across her forehead. No matter how many times Mac had tried to talk Eve out of going with him to the rendezvous sight, she'd insisted.

They moved along the rocky ground until they neared a drop-off leading downward into the river valley. With the sun below the horizon now, the clouds snuffed out the remaining rays. The only light illuminating the sky was the increasingly more frequent flashes of lightning. Mac switched on his flashlight and shone it into the black abyss that was the hollowed out riverbed. Because of the recent drought, the river was nothing more than a five-foot-wide stream easily traversed down the middle. He descended into the river bottom and guided his horse upriver until bluffs towered on either side of them. The limestone walls were riddled with crevices, leading to a beehive of caverns within the hills. Mac had played in these caves as a boy, scaring up bats and small animals.

Large, lazy drops of rain smacked him in the face and plopped into the water. The first few drops were more an annoyance than a hindrance. But the single fat drops turned into many, and soon they were moving through a downpour.

Mac stopped his horse and waved Eve forward. Water streamed off his hat, but he could see all right.

Eve was drenched, her hair plastered to her face and neck. "Why are we stopping?"

"We're here." He pointed up at a steep embankment leading to a ledge thirty feet above the river. "We need to hurry. We have to get out of the riverbed."

"Why?"

"Even though it hasn't been raining for very long, it could be raining harder upstream," Mac yelled over the noise of the downpour. "We might get caught in a flash flood."

Eve's eyes widened, but her lips firmed. "Then let's get up there. I hope she's already there. Otherwise, she might not get here tonight."

Through the drenching rain, Mac kicked his horse's flanks and jerked his reins to the side, sending his horse up the embankment. The horse's hooves slipped in the mud and he struggled to gain purchase. Eventually he did and continued the climb.

With one hand on the reins, Mac balanced a flashlight in the other, making broad, sweeping arcs, frustrated at the pathetic band of light it created. If Cynthia were out here, they wouldn't see her until they were upon her.

Another blaze of lightning revealed something white on the ground ahead. Mac's heart rate sprang into a gallop. Could it be Cynthia? Like a strobe, the sky blinked, illuminating the path. With his stomach tightening with each *clip-clop* of the horse's hooves, Mac eased forward.

The white lump lay in a twisted heap. *Please don't be Cynthia.*

Glad his horse blocked Eve's view, Mac strained to make out what was on the ground. Blood pumped through his veins in jolting bursts. Not until his horse stood directly over it could he make out what the lump was. And it wasn't the girl.

Mac blew out a stream of air, realizing he'd held his breath from the time he'd spotted the dead animal to the time he identified it as a calf.

A small brown and white Hereford lay in a mangled pile of hide and bones.

Eve pulled her horse up behind him and stood in her stirrups. "What is it?"

"A calf," he shouted over his shoulder. He

moved his horse farther down the trail to allow Eve a view of the carcass.

In the light from the flashlight and the lightning, her face appeared pale, her shoulders stiff. "What happened to it?" Before Mac could answer, she came to the same conclusion he had. "The creature did it." Her words weren't a question but a flat statement. The quaver in her voice said more than what was spoken. She was terrified Cynthia would end up like this.

The wind picked up, whipping stinging rain into their eyes and making further movement nearly impossible.

They had to make it to the cave soon. A huge spark, followed by an enormous bang, ripped the air.

Mac's horse reared. The flashlight fell from his hands. Using all his skill and strength, he struggled to stay in the saddle. When he calmed the horse to a nervous dance, he shot a glance back to Eve. Without a flashlight he had to wait for another lightning bolt to illuminate the trail.

A burst of lightning fractured the sky and revealed an empty trail. Horse and rider were gone!

"Eve!" Mac spun his bay gelding around, ready to gallop back the way they'd come when he heard a faint cry.

"Mac, I'm here."

The sound came from the ground beside the trail.

As he slid from his saddle, Mac cursed the darkness. "Eve?" He felt around the rock-strewn earth, working his way down the trail until he clasped an outstretched hand. "Damn it, Eve." He crushed her to his chest. "You scared the life out of me."

"Not so tight, I'm a little bruised from the fall."

Mac immediately loosened his hold and felt along her limbs. "Anything hurt?" He panned the area for the flashlight and spotted it three feet away, still glowing. He reached for it and shined it in her face.

Eve raised a hand to block the beam. "Hey, easy on the eyes. I got a bit of a bump on the back of my head and a few bruises, but I don't think anything's broken."

He pressed a hand to her cheek and felt around the back of her head. As she'd indicated, there was a small bump beneath her hair. "We need to get you back. You could have a concussion."

"I'm okay." She struggled to stand. "We have to find Cynthia."

He helped her to her feet, circling an arm around her waist to steady her. "We should go back to town."

"Not without Cynthia." She pulled away from his hands and stood shivering in the rain. "Now, where's my horse?"

Mac smiled at her strength and determination. "He's long gone. Probably halfway back to the barn by now."

"Then we'll have to ride double," she stated. "I can't go back until we know one way or another." Tears streamed down her face, and her shoulders shook with silent sobs.

The clouds chose that moment to dump their contents in earnest, blinding them in their intensity. Within seconds, the path became a river.

Mac grabbed Eve's elbow to steady her, yelling above the pounding torrent, "We're almost there. Come on." His heart squeezing a little tighter, he hurried her toward his horse. The animal's eyes rolled wildly with each crash of thunder. He danced on the narrow path almost knocking Eve to the ground.

Snatching the reins, Mac shook his head at Eve. "We'll have to walk from here."

As if to emphasize Mac's point, a slash of lightning struck a tree a hundred yards ahead of them, setting it ablaze. Thunder followed immediately, the nearness and force shaking the earth. Mac held tight to the reins, but the horse reared. "Look out!" he shouted. The frenzied animal backed into Eve, knocking her to the muddy trail.

Struggling to hold the horse from trampling her, Mac strained to see through the blinding rain and dark. He was so scared for her, he couldn't breathe. "Eve? Eve?"

"I'm okay," she cried faintly.

Mac had enough. He turned the horse around, lifted Eve up with one arm around her middle and hobbled, pushed and tramped up the hill. If his memory served him right, the cave opening would be just ahead. It was large enough to let two very wet people in to keep safe and dry. It also had an overhang of rocks large enough to provide shelter for his horse. Where was it?

The lightning strobed with enough wattage to illuminate an outcropping of rocks smothered in fresh-growth cedar and prickly pear cactus. Mac wasn't sure. The entrance didn't look quite the same as it had the last time he'd been there, over ten years ago.

Mac leaned close until his mouth practically touched Eve's ear. "Can you stand by yourself?"

"Yes."

"Hold this." He shoved the flashlight into her hand, then led the horse through the bramble. Bingo. He found the opening he'd hoped for and a solid rock surface with a little bit of an overhang for his horse. Mac tied the horse to a cedar sapling and dashed back out into the storm.

Eve stood, a bedraggled waif, just where he'd left her, the beam of the flashlight pointed toward him. Lightning crashed nonstop, providing enough light to fool a person into thinking it was just a cold, wet morning in Texas.

When Mac grabbed her hand and pulled her toward the cave, she stumbled and nearly fell at his feet. Without a word, he scooped her in his arms and tromped up the slight incline to the cave, ducking into the entrance just as another rumbling bout of thunder shook the ground.

As soon as he stepped through the opening, the rain that had pounded in his ears became a steady rumble outside. Inside the underground shelter, all was quiet. The cave smelled of damp rock and the musty sulfuric aroma of minerals dripping through seams in the earth's crust.

He set Eve on her feet and held her around the waist, resting his forehead against hers. Finally able to breathe, he dragged in air to fill his lungs.

Eve wobbled beneath his arms, her skin cold and wet. She pulled back enough to look around. "She's not here, Mac. Where could she be?"

"I don't know. For all we know she's safe and sound drinking cocoa and eating cookies with Jess," Mac said, although he was sure that wasn't the case. He felt around for his cell phone, certain the little device would be completely useless after he'd fallen so many times in the rain and mud. But two little service bars glowed green in the night. Mac moved closer to the opening and a third bar blinked green.

Within seconds he'd dialed Addie's number.

"Has anyone seen or heard from Cynthia?" Mac asked.

"By that I guess you didn't find her?" Addie sighed into the phone. "No. We haven't seen hide nor hair."

"Is Joey okay?" Eve leaned into the cell phone.

"Tell Eve Joey's having a fine time over at Katie's. I left there a few minutes ago and Laura was busy fixin' mac-n-cheese for the kids."

Eve laughed, tears welling in her eyes. "Thank you."

"Addie, the storm's pretty bad right now. We're going to stay put until it passes. If Cynthia should call, get the sheriff. We have to find her."

"You got it, Mac. I'll be watchin' for her. By the way, there's flash flood warnings for the county until two in the morning. You two take care. That river's been known to rise all of a sudden. Don't get caught by surprise."

Mac flipped his cell phone shut and told Eve about the flash flood warning. "Looks like we're stuck here for a little while until the storm dies down." He stared into her eyes. "Are you going to be all right for a minute? I want to get the saddle off the horse."

"Don't worry about me. I'm fine."

Mac hesitated, his eyes narrowing. Then he nodded and ducked back outside into the storm.

WHILE SHE WAITED for him to return, Eve held her breath. She shouldn't be nervous in a cave by herself. Mac was only a few steps away. But she couldn't help the eerie feeling the cave inspired.

In the minute he'd promised, Mac was back, tossing the saddle and blanket to the ground.

Eve released her pent-up breath and rubbed her arms. A shiver coursed down her back, raising gooseflesh on her skin. She didn't know whether the shiver was from the cold or from the fact that she'd be spending the next couple of hours alone with Mac. Was it possible to be cold and completely on fire at the same time? A shudder racked her body and her teeth clattered. Okay, so she was officially cold.

"You're freezing." Mac reached for her.

Eve backed away, not sure she could handle his closeness. The last time he'd held her, she thought she'd burst into flames, their passions had flared to scorching. "I'll be all right. It's not

really that cold. It's just my clothes. They're…"
As if of their own accord, her teeth rattled
against each other.

"…soaking wet," he finished for her.

"You've b-been such a g-good Boy Scout, I
don't s-suppose, you have dry clothes for me to
change into?" She tried to smile, but the stress
of the past hour on horseback must have shown.

Mac held out his arms. "Come here."

"I'll b-be all right. I'm just a little tired."

"I'll bet you're a little scared and probably
shocky after that fall from your horse." He
closed the distance between them and tipped
her face up. "I promise not to do anything you
don't want to. Just let me hold you to get you
warm." He peeled her jacket off her arms, one
sleeve at a time.

"I don't know if it's such a good idea…."
Why was she fighting him, when she was only
delaying the inevitable? She wanted to be in this
man's arms.

"Look, Eve, I know how you feel about Joey
and I'm not trying to horn in on your life. But
let me warm you up. We may be here a while."

Eve gave in and leaned against him. "Only
because I'm cold."

"I know." His arms wrapped around her
waist, pulling her body up against his.

For a moment they stood in silence, letting the heat of their two bodies warm each other.

His breath stirred the hair next to her ear and she could swear his lips brushed against her earlobe.

Before she could think, before she could rationalize, her arms slid up around Mac's neck. She tugged him down to her and skimmed her lips across his in a soft, tentative kiss. "I don't know what you do to me, but I wish you'd stop." Her actions belying her words, Eve kissed him hard.

This time he returned the pressure, his palm at the base of her spine pulling her closer until the hard evidence of his desire pressed against her belly. He broke contact with her lips only enough to whisper, "You want me to stop?"

"No. But what about Cynthia?"

"We'd be foolish to leave shelter in this storm. And Cynthia won't be able to find the cave in the rain and the dark."

"But we should be out looking."

"Not with the lightning as bad as it is."

A thunderous boom echoed through the cave, emphasizing Mac's point.

She was afraid for Cynthia and she was afraid for herself. How could she come out of an encounter with Mac unscathed? He wasn't a man a woman could easily forget. In a cold, dark cave, cut off from the rest of the world by a violent storm, Eve needed him now, more than she could resist. "I'm scared, Mac."

"Me, too." He tipped her chin up and claimed her lips, his tongue sliding between her teeth to tangle with hers. With slow, deft hands, he pulled her T-shirt up and over her head, leaving her standing in sopping jeans and a lacy bra.

Her fingers worked the buttons of his shirt, starting at the top and inching their way down to where his shirt disappeared into the waistband of his jeans. With her hand hovering over the large metal button, she glanced up. Did she dare?

"You don't have to do this," he reminded her. His dark gaze bore into hers.

Eve inhaled a deep breath and blew it out. "I want to."

A smile spread across his face and white teeth shone in the pale glow of the flashlight. "You don't know how often I've thought about doing just this."

"Really?" The heat of his gaze warmed her chilled skin. Eve tipped her head to the side. "You should smile more often."

His smile slipped then completely disappeared. "Have to have something to smile about."

"I know." She wanted to smooth away the lines from his forehead, take away his torment.

Love him until he forgot all the horrors of the war. Her hands worked the button loose on his jeans and she slid the zipper down.

Another shiver shook her from head to foot. She hadn't been with a man since her ex-husband over two years ago. Eve knew if she went into Mac's arms, she'd never be the same.

"I don't need another man in my life, though." Her voice was little more than a whisper. Not in the least convincing. Who was she trying to fool?

"But you need warmth, Eve," he said, his voice deep and raspy. "And I need you. Come here." He stepped closer, leaving a little space between them.

If she wanted his warmth, she'd have to make the next move. Like a leaf sucked over the edge of a cliff by a strong gust of wind, she fell into his arms, unable and unwilling to refuse to give in to this attraction any longer.

Why should she? Her body had natural desires and longings. Giving into them wasn't going against her self-imposed ban on marriage. He was deliciously warm. Everywhere his skin touched hers nerve endings ignited, sending shock waves to her core.

With a trembling hand, she pulled his head down to hers until her lips were but a breath away from his. "My first impression was right."

He brushed his tongue across her mouth, sending tingling thrills throughout her body. "And what was that?"

"You're dangerous, Mac McGuire. Sinfully dangerous." Then she claimed his mouth, diving in to tease his tongue. Her body pressed against his. She couldn't get enough. His heat drew her closer. She wouldn't survive this time together without being singed, maybe torched. But suddenly she didn't care. All she wanted was to be in Mac's arms. Let tomorrow figure itself out.

When Mac eased her jeans down over her hips, she didn't fight it, she stood trembling in the dark, damp cave, reveling in the feel of his fingers against her thighs. When they both stood facing each other in nothing but their underwear, she began to question her sanity.

But Mac pulled her into his arms and held her close, his lips pressed against her ear. "We don't have to go any further. Say the word and I stop here."

The choice was in her hands. If she were stronger and stuck to her guns, she'd tell him to stop. Where Mac was concerned, she had no willpower. With shaking hands, she pulled his face down to hers and kissed his lips. "Please, Mac, don't stop."

He hesitated only a moment longer, before he pushed his fingers under the elastic of her panties and, in one smooth stroke, he pushed them from her hips and down her thighs, his hand blazing a path to her ankles.

Eve shivered, not from cold, but from delicious anticipation. She touched the edge of his briefs.

With an indrawn breath, Mac grasped her hands and held them still. "Don't start something you can't finish."

She pushed her shoulders back, having made her decision. "I'm okay, Mac. Let me."

Then she slid his briefs to the ground, letting her hands glide over the coarse hairs curling along his thighs and calves. The muscles beneath were taut, bulging with strength, and his manhood swelled in proud magnificence. He was gorgeous.

Aching with longing, she rose to stand in front of him, reaching behind her back to unclasp her bra, her breasts spilling free.

Mac inhaled and let out his breath in a shaky stream. "Eve, I don't deserve you."

Her brows creased and she stepped closer, her breasts touching his chest. "Yes, you do and so much more. You're a good man, Mac."

With a sigh, he pulled her into his arms and held her naked skin against his. She could do this all night. Hell, she could do this for the rest of her life.

Sanity tried to slip one last road bump into her mind. "What about tomorrow?"

He kissed the tip of her nose, the erogenous zone behind her ear, "What about tomorrow?" His lips claimed hers before she could answer.

Tomorrow, she decided, was another day. She rev-eled in the here and now. Home might as well be a hundred miles away with the storm pounding outside—never mind the storm raging within. Lightning bolts flashed in rhythm with the internal electric charges radiating downward. If she didn't have him soon, she would come apart at the seams, unraveling into a billion pieces.

Mac ran his hands around her back and down over her buttocks, tracing a line to her inner thigh. He lifted her, fitting her legs around his waist, and slowly lowered her until she hovered over his jutting erection.

Her body pulsed, willing him to fill her. She couldn't understand why he stopped.

In the soft glow of the flashlight long forgotten on the cave's dirt floor, Mac's eyes glowed charcoal-gray with the intensity of his concentration, almost strain. "We don't have protection."

With his velvety tip nudging against her

entrance, promising relief, Eve groaned. "Damn the bastions, full steam ahead." She pushed downward, taking him fully into her, relishing the searing heat and rigid strength. He felt so good, filling her tight walls until she thought she would burst. With her hands braced on his shoulders, she eased upward and then lifted and lowered steadily.

"I can't fight you anymore, Eve. I need you as much as the air I breathe." He pushed harder into her until skin slapped against skin, the noises echoing off the cave walls.

Eve tensed, squeezed her eyes shut and exploded into a kaleidoscope of colors, a sunburst in the darkened cave.

Mac thrust one last time and held her tight against him, before lifting her up and off him in time for his release.

Somewhere back in her sorry excuse for gray matter, Eve realized the importance of Mac's move and loved him all the more for it.

Love?

Her arms circled Mac's neck as he slid her down his body in a slow descent to set her upright. When her feet hit bottom, even the chill of the cold, hard earth couldn't dispel the heat they'd generated.

But love?

"Are you okay?" Mac's breath stirred the drying hairs next to her ear.

Afraid to lift her head for fear he'd see in her face something she wasn't ready to admit even to herself, Eve pressed her cheek into his rock-hard chest. She languished against his taut skin, twirling her fingers into the curly hairs around his hard brown nipples. His salt, leather and aftershave scent lightly teased her senses, imprinting on her memory.

How could she have let herself do this? She knew, firsthand, the risks of bringing a stepparent into a family. She couldn't bring that kind of grief to Joey. He'd had enough already.

But would Mac be different than her own stepfather? Hadn't he already proven he could be patient with Joey? Hadn't he just proven he respected her enough not to think of only his needs?

Her fingers tightened and tugged a little too hard, pulling his hairs.

"Ouch!" Mac's body jerked and his hand skimmed her naked back. "Careful there."

"I'm sorry." She worked her hand free, her face filling with heat. She made the mistake of looking up into Mac's laughing warm gray-blue eyes.

How could she remain aloof and lead a separate life from this wonderful, caring man? Especially when all she wanted to do was have a repeat performance of what they'd just done...for the rest of her life.

Boy, they were in trouble. Her with her hang-ups about her stepfather, Joey traumatized by his father's death and Mac still recovering from war wounds—it was all too much for her to deal with. "Mac?"

"Yeah, baby?"

"What happened in Iraq?" As soon as the question popped out, she regretted it. Why couldn't she leave well enough alone?

Mac's shoulders tensed and he stared over her head at the faded drawings on the cave wall. "We were hit by a roadside bomb." His eyes narrowed as if pain shot through his head. "I was wounded and knocked unconscious. When I came to, all of my men were dead." The last sentence was stated in a flat, emotionless tone.

Eve placed a hand over his heart. "Except you."

When he started to pull away, Eve wouldn't let him. She locked her arms around his waist and held on, pressing her face into the curve of his neck. "You know, you can't go on blaming yourself for what happened." Her words were whispered against his ear with the gentleness of a caress.

Mac stood stiff, unmoving. "They died, I didn't," he said, his voice a harsh staccato.

Her heart squeezing tight in her chest, Eve ached to take away his pain. Without thinking, she reached up and cupped his cheek with her hand. "You can't change the past, nor remain buried in it. It'll only ruin any chance of a future."

His lips firmed into a line before he shoved a hand through his hair. "It's hard not to."

Eve's eyes misted as she struggled with the truth of her words and his. Had she been projecting her stepfather onto every man she'd met since her divorce? "My stepfather was hateful and verbally abusive," she admitted softly.

"I'm not your stepfather, and I care for you and Joey—more than I wanted to." His hands moved up to grip her arms. "I don't have much to offer and I come with a whole lot of baggage, but I'm hoping, with love and time, I'll overcome it. I'm just missing one ingredient."

Eve pressed a hand to his mouth. "No, don't say it. Don't." She feared he would voice what she had been thinking only moments before. "You don't understand. My stepfather didn't love me." With her forehead leaning against his bare chest, she fought for control. "I wasn't his flesh and blood. He only wanted my mother, and I was in the way. I was a little girl and I only wanted to be loved. Instead he made my life miserable. I can't do that to Joey. If that means sacrificing my needs and desires, I have to do it." She stared up at Mac, tears spilling over and coursing down her cheeks. "My son deserves to be loved not rejected."

For a long moment, Mac stared down at her, then he sighed and pulled her stiffening body against his. "Don't worry. I won't mess up your life." Pulling her closer, he skimmed his lips across her temple. "Why don't we let tomorrow sort things out? For now we need each other to stay warm. At least until the storm stops."

The storm.

Through her drying tears, Eve listened for the sound of thunder and the steady roar of rain. "Do you hear that?"

With his ear cocked toward the cave entrance, Mac stilled, his arms resting around her naked waist. "The storm stopped."

Chapter Fourteen

The trip back to the ranch was slow and treacherous. Riding double with Eve behind him, Mac was sure to go easy so as not to lose her again.

All the while she rode with her arms around his waist, Mac marveled at how close they were and yet how wide the chasm between them had grown. Determined to face one problem at a time, he pushed his own needs and desires to the side and focused his concentration on finding Cynthia. But Eve's arms around him and her warmth against his back blurred his focus.

Although the rain had stopped, the cloud cover continued to hold back any light that might have shone down on them from the moon and stars. Mac hadn't seen the night sky in so many days he couldn't remember what phase of the moon they were in.

Once at the ranch, he and Eve transferred

to the truck, loaded Molly in the bed and headed for town.

The silence inside the truck was palpable. He'd left Eve to her thoughts on the ride back, not sure if further rehashing of their situation would scare her off. But the silence was killing him. "Eve?"

"Hmm?" She leaned against the far door, the side of her head resting against the window.

"Just so you know…" He swallowed the lump threatening to close off his vocal chords. "I'm not giving up on you."

She sat up straight and turned to look at him. In the light from the dash, her green eyes shone like the richest emeralds, dark circles smudged the pale skin beneath her eyes. A wrinkle settled between her eyes and she chewed on her lower lip. "I can't guarantee a future with you, Mac."

"I know and I don't expect it." He stared straight ahead. "I just wanted you to know I'm not giving up on you."

Mac dared another quick glance her way.

Now she was staring straight ahead, fat tears trembling on her lashes.

When they arrived on Main Street, the area in front of the General Store was a mass of cars, trucks and people armed with flashlights and rifles.

Mac parked the truck a block away. "Wonder what's happening."

"Let's find out." Eve slipped from the truck and hurried forward, pushing her way through the crowd to get to where Addie and Sheriff Hodges stood on the steps of the porch.

Mac followed. "What's going on?" he asked Addie.

"After you called, I put a call in to Jess Harding. He still hadn't seen Cynthia and sounded kinda funny about it. I figured it was time to call the law." Addie nodded to Sheriff Hodges.

"Ms. Addie told me about what happened at the river caves," the sheriff said. "We're organizing a search party."

"Jess Harding might not be worried enough about his daughter to join us, but the rest of us are here." Addie crossed her arms over her chest, her lips pressing together into a thin line. "We haven't seen her since noon. And no one has seen Toby."

Sheriff Hodges turned to address the dozen men standing in the light spilling from the General Store. "If we split up we can cover more ground."

In the space of ten minutes, each group of men, armed with cell phones and walkie-talkies, was given a sector of the county to search. The small crowd dispersed to their assigned locations, leaving the sheriff, Mac, Eve and Addie the only people on the front porch of the store.

"I'm headed over to the hill where the teenagers like to make out," the sheriff said. "Mac, could you check one more time out at the Harding place to see if Jess has seen Cynthia? I tried calling but Jess isn't answering."

"Yeah. I'll go."

"*We'll* go," Eve corrected.

Mac looked down at the woman next to him. She'd conquered the fear of traveling through the night on horseback, survived a wicked storm and a man's attentions she swore she couldn't allow. Yet, Eve still cared enough about a child, not even her own, that she'd risk her life yet again to help.

"I got a bad feeling about this, Mac." Sheriff Hodges shook his head. "The state crime lab's preliminary reports revealed that Art Nantan was killed in an animal attack."

"Animal, huh?" Mac's lips pressed together. The dead calf on the trail up to the cave flashed through his mind. "For once, I almost hope we find Cynthia with Toby. We'll head out to Jess's. If anything comes up, you can reach me by cell phone."

MAC HAD BEEN QUIET since they'd left the store, his thoughts tumbling around all that had happened, from the discovery of the dead animals to what had happened back in the cave.

"Do you think we'll find her tonight?" Eve broke through the quiet in the cab of the pickup.

"I hope we do, before something happens." Mac's jaw tightened as he stared straight ahead. He slammed his palm against the steering wheel. "Where could she be?"

With every passing hour, Mac's fear for Cynthia grew until it was a burning sense of urgency building in his chest. It was already past midnight, and no one had seen Toby or Cynthia.

At the Harding place there wasn't a single light on.

"You don't think Jess went to bed knowing Cynthia hasn't been found, do you?" Eve asked.

Mac shook his head, afraid if he opened his mouth he'd let out the string of curses he wanted to say. Jess hadn't been on the ball where his daughter was concerned.

Just as he opened the door to the pickup, Molly jumped out of the back and raced toward the house.

"That's odd." Mac shoved his door open and climbed down. "She usually doesn't jump out of the truck until I let her."

The dog leaped up on the porch and pressed her nose to the boards, pacing the front of the house from one end to the other, growling softly with each step. She stopped at the door and scratched. When the door didn't open, she scratched again. Molly looked back at Mac, a soulful look on her face in the light from the pickup. With a whimper, she went back to scratching at the door.

"Here, let me." Mac knocked on the door. When no one responded, he tried the door handle. It turned freely and the door swung open.

Before he could grab her by the scruff of her neck, Molly darted inside.

Mac called her and went in after her. "Jess? Anyone home?" He flicked the light switch on the wall and blinked at the brightness.

Eve gasped beside him. "Oh my God."

With a pistol shoved into his mouth, Jess Harding's lifeless form lay sprawled on the couch.

Molly lay on the floor next to the couch with her head on her front paws, whimpering.

"Damn." Mac spun, grabbed Eve by her shoulders and pressed her to his chest. "Come on. You can sit in the truck while I call the sheriff."

"No, I'm okay." Her body belied her words. Mac could feel her trembling.

"Please, Eve, go sit in the truck."

She leaned back just far enough to look up into his eyes. "I'm okay." Then she pushed away from him and walked into the room, her face white but her jaw set firmly. "Was it suicide? Or do you think someone killed him and made it look like suicide?" She didn't stare at Jess; instead she glanced around the room.

"That's for the forensics team to decide. I'll call the sheriff." Mac patted his pockets for his cell phone until he remembered he'd left it on the seat of his pickup. Instead of retracing his steps back to get his cell, he made his way across the room to the telephone on the counter. As he reached for the phone, he noticed a white sheet of paper lying next to it.

The handwriting was a jerky scrawl, but Mac could read the words clearly. As he did, a cold hand squeezed his chest.

Beware the wolf among us. God help me, I can't live in fear anymore.

"Eve, look at this."

Eve strode across the room, her gaze carefully averted from the body on the couch and the blood pooled on the floor.

He handed her the paper and stared at her while she read.

Her face paled and when she finished, her gaze met his, confused and scared.

"What does this mean? Whom is he referring to?"

"I don't know. But based on this note, I'd guess this was suicide." Mac lifted the phone and dialed the sheriff's cell phone number. After he'd given all the information he hung up.

"We need to find Cynthia." Eve stared down at the note. "Think she might be out at Toby's place?"

"I don't know, but it's worth a try."

"What about waiting for the sheriff?"

"Jess can't be saved." Mac laid the note on the counter where he'd found it. "We need to find Cynthia."

"I agree. Let's go."

At Toby's house, no one was home and the door was locked.

"Where would they have gone?" Mac questioned himself out loud as he pulled out of the yard and headed back out to the highway.

"I don't know but maybe that's Toby now." Eve pointed at the lights bumping along Toby's rutted driveway.

With the finesse of a prizefighter, Mac slammed his shift into Park, throwing the two occupants in the cab against their seat belts. Before Eve could mouth a protest, Mac leaped to the ground, striding toward the slowing vehicle. "Toby Rice, get down out of that truck."

"What are you doin' on my property?" Toby

leaned out the window, and then opened the door, all but falling to the ground. A dark brown beer bottle rolled out of the truck and crashed against a rock, shattering into a million pieces.

Mac grabbed the younger man by the collar and hauled him to his feet. His breath reeked like the inside of a brewery, and his eyes were glassy and bloodshot. "Where's Cynthia?"

"Don't know. Don't care." Toby scowled at Mac. "What's it to ya?"

For a moment, Mac held Toby up by the collar. Then all the frustration exploded inside him. He slugged Toby in the mouth with one hand, holding him up with the other. "Tell me where she is."

Toby's head rolled back then straightened. "You gonna hit me again? If so, I'm not saying a word."

Still holding the younger man's collar, Mac bunched his fist to throw another punch.

Eve's hand on his shoulder stopped him.

"Mac, let him go." Eve peeled Mac's fingers from Toby and placed herself between the two men. "Look, Toby, the entire town is out looking for Cynthia. We're worried about her. She hasn't been seen since before noon. The sheriff's been out combing the county for her and he's convinced she would be with you. Since she isn't, you'd better tell us where she is."

"He's got no right hitting me." Toby rubbed his fist across a bloody lip. "Keep that jerk away from me."

Mac breathed in and breathed out like a fighting bull, his fist still clenched, barely in control.

Eve tipped her head toward Mac. "I don't know that I can guarantee anything. Mac has been fighting in the streets of Iraq recently and he might be demonstrating a little bit of post-traumatic shock syndrome. No telling what he'll do if I turn him loose on you."

Toby looked at Mac and stepped back.

Good, let the idiot think he had mental issues. Mac's hand already hurt from connecting with the big jerk's bony jaw. He needed to save his energy for finding Cynthia.

"Are you going to tell us where Cynthia is, or should I let Mac show you how he was trained to interrogate a prisoner?" Eve's voice dropped low. "Special Forces style."

"Look, I ain't afraid of him." Toby's words didn't match the fear reflected in his face. "And I ain't got no information on that slut."

"Eve, we're wasting time. Let me at him." Mac tried to shove her aside, but Eve stood firm.

"Okay, okay. She and I had a fight a couple hours ago. We were down by the river bridge and she wouldn't get back in the truck. Said she'd walk home." He shrugged. "So I let her."

"You let her walk home alone? In the dark? And it was raining at that time." Mac's voice was a growl. Anger boiled up inside him until he felt as if he would explode. The situation was worse than Mac thought and his gut told him it wasn't getting better.

"It had stopped raining by the time she took off. Besides, why should I care? She wouldn't get in the truck. What was I supposed to do, throw her in?"

"It wouldn't be the first time," Mac said. "Move, Eve. I'll only hurt him a little."

"Wait." Eve shoved Mac back. "So where have you been for the past few hours, Toby?"

"I stayed by the river, shootin' at beer bottles."

"And drinking. While Cynthia walked home alone." Eve's voice was quiet, reasonable. Then she stepped aside. "Have at him, Mac."

Toby's eyes rounded.

Mac bunched his fist, but before he could swing at Toby, Eve landed a hardpacked punch to Toby's gut.

The redneck doubled over, gasping for breath.

Mac's eyes widened and he stared down at the amazing woman next to him. "Remind me not to make you mad." Then he shoved his hand through his hair, that edgy feeling pushing his heart rate faster. "Get in my truck, Toby," he ordered.

"I ain't goin' nowhere with you two." He wheezed several times, attempting to straighten.

Mac pushed him against the hood of the Ford. "You're getting in the truck and showing us where you last saw Cynthia."

"And who's gonna make me?" He looked up at Mac and Eve and then down at their bunched fists. "Okay, okay. Although I don't know what good it's gonna do. She's probably back at her papa's place by now."

"She's not. We just came from there." Mac paused before saying, "We found Jess Harding dead."

"What?" Toby's eyes widened.

"You heard me. Now get in." Mac shoved him into the truck. "We don't have time to waste arguing."

Eve called the sheriff on her cell phone, letting him know they'd found Toby and where they were headed.

Throughout the drive to the river, Mac ground his teeth. He had the same feeling just before his troops had been ambushed. That same feeling that something's not right or something bad was about to happen. And he felt just as frustrated and helpless to stop the tragedy from unfolding. The feeling came too late last time. He just prayed he wasn't too late this time.

Toby directed them down a dirt path that led to the river below the highway bridge.

"She took off walkin' from here. Her papa's house is on the other side of that field and over the hill." He stood on the gravel and pointed up the slope toward an open field. "Now what're you gonna do?"

"*We* are going to search until *we* find her." Mac grabbed Toby's arm and dragged him out of the truck.

The younger man stumbled and planted his boots in the gravel. "I ain't walkin' nowhere in the dark. No tellin' what's out there."

"But you let Cynthia walk alone in the dark?" Mac shook his head. "They have ways of dealing with people like you back in Iraq."

Toby crossed his arms over his barrel chest. "Yeah, well, we're not in Iraq."

"Too bad. You're coming with us." Mac grabbed the flashlight from beneath the truck seat, walked to the rear of the vehicle and dropped the tailgate. "Come, Molly." The dog leaped to the ground and trotted alongside Mac and Eve.

Several sets of headlights bounced down the

rutted track, led by the flashing lights of the sheriff's SUV.

Townsfolk climbed from trucks and cars and stood around in the muck awaiting orders. Mac scanned faces he knew. Tom Taylor, Hank Bleumfeld, Bernie Odom and even Mayor Logan.

The mayor stepped forward, a serious look on his face, his hand outstretched. "We're here to help."

Mac glanced down at the man's hand and ignored it. "Then form a line."

Sheriff Hodges emerged from his vehicle and strode across the gravel to Mac. "I've called for the tracking dogs." He stared over at the sullen Toby, who was scuffing the ground with the toe of his dirty cowboy boots. "Think Toby's done something stupid?"

Mac stared up the hill. "Letting her walk out there alone was about as stupid as you get."

The sheriff's brows drew downward and he cocked his head to the side. "And we thought we'd gotten the animals responsible for the attacks on the local livestock. Until Art's and Jess's deaths, I didn't think we were dealing with anything but four-legged animals. Looks like there are the two-legged types involved as well."

His lips pressed together, Mac didn't respond.

"Let's hope she doesn't get worse than a snakebite or a broken leg," the sheriff said, shooting Toby a hard stare.

"She should be so lucky." Mac's shoulders tensed and the knot in his gut tightened.

"Look, I'll leave a deputy here to wait for the tracking dogs." Hodges nodded at Molly. "Is your animal trained to track at all?"

"Yeah." Mac patted Molly's head and scratched behind her ears. "Sheriff, we need to move. I have the feeling we're running out of time."

"Then let's get this show on the road." He handed Mac a jacket. "This is Cynthia's. Let's see what the dog can find."

Mac knelt beside Molly and held the garment in front of the animal's nose. She sniffed, her stump wagging in tight, excited flicks.

"Find." Mac stood and waved his hand toward the hill. "Find."

Without a backward glance, Molly sprang forward and bounded up the embankment.

Sheriff Hodges organized the men into a line within shouting distance of each other, spreading out as they had done to find the hogs.

Mac turned to Toby. "You're coming with me."

"You can't make me go anywhere. Ain't that right, Sheriff?"

"Toby, you better do as you're told. I could write you up for kidnapping and assault. And depending on what we find—and God help us we don't—possibly murder. Not to mention, I still have a few questions for you concerning the deaths of Art Nantan and Jess Harding."

The color left Toby's face. "I ain't killed nobody. You can't pin nothing on me."

"Right this minute we got two dead men and a missing girl, and the last one to see Cynthia was you. That makes you our prime suspect."

"I didn't give her anything she didn't deserve." Toby stood firm, refusing to go with Mac.

Eve walked up behind Mac and grabbed his arm. "We need to go. We can't waste time on that loser."

After placing one of his deputies in charge of Toby, Sheriff Hodges jogged to the line of men and then turned toward the field. "Let's go."

Mac moved quickly following Molly up the hill and across an open field, occasionally breaking into a run to keep the dog in sight.

The human chain crossed the field and entered a wooded area full of live oaks and scrub cedar. The smaller bushes crowded the path making progress slow and painful. Mac, staying close to Eve, soon lost sight of Molly.

"Sheriff?" The static-filled sound of a police radio disturbed the darkness.

"Yeah, Bill?" Sheriff Hodges replied, coming to a stop.

Mac and Eve paused alongside him.

"Toby got away, sir," Bill's voice sounded breathless and tired. "He plowed into me like a freakin' linebacker and disappeared into the dark before I could pick myself up out of the dirt."

"Damn." The sheriff rubbed his chin and stared ahead where Molly had gone. With a sigh, he pressed the button on his radio. "Can't be helped now. Why don't you go stake out his place and see if he shows up?"

"Yes, sir."

His mouth set in a grim line, the sheriff motioned Eve and Mac forward to rejoin the search line. "Come on, we got a girl to find."

Before they'd taken more than a dozen steps into the black night, excited barking erupted through the thick growth of cedar.

"She's found her." Mac crashed through the brush, cedar branches scratching and tearing at his face and arms.

Just as he cleared the wooded area and emerged into another field, the barking stopped.

An eerie howl filled the night air.

Damn. Mac's gut clenched and he slowed to

a walk, no longer anxious to find Cynthia. When Eve moved up beside him, he clasped her hand in his. He didn't want her to see what he knew they'd find.

Chapter Fifteen

Eve hadn't moved from the circle of Mac's arms since they'd discovered Cynthia's body. No matter how hard she tried, she couldn't quit shaking. If not for Mac, she'd have collapsed into worthless hysteria by now.

The heavy pall of clouds clogged the sky the entire day in Spirit Canyon, setting a fitting mood for the town's loss. The media, state police, homicide detectives and the morbid curiosity seekers crawled the streets, asking questions and snapping pictures of the townsfolk in their shock and disbelief.

Throughout the ordeal, Eve spoke to the police detectives and listened as others did the same, her thoughts mired in visions of Cynthia lying in a twisted heap.

How could this have happened? Cynthia was a nice girl. She didn't deserve to die, especially such a horrific death.

Near the end of the day, the ebb of people flowed out of their little town, and still Mac and Eve hadn't taken a break to eat or sleep. Just when Eve thought she couldn't take any more, Mac walked her to the sheriff's office. The old jailhouse was a two-story limestone building that looked like it had been built when the town was established over a hundred years ago.

"We'll check in with the sheriff and then we'll go get Joey," he told her.

Joey. Eve focused on thoughts of her son. With all the bad creeping in around her, Joey represented all the good that life had to offer. She'd left him in Laura's care to spare him the ugliness of people talking openly about Cynthia's death.

But now she wanted to be with her son. To hold him close and reassure herself that he was alive and healthy.

"Mac, Eve, good to see you two." Mayor Logan stepped in front of them before they reached the jailhouse door.

"Mayor Logan." Eve acknowledged the man when Mac didn't.

"A sad thing, our little Cynthia. Such a waste." He shook his head, his brows wrinkling over his blue-gray eyes. "I heard you were there when they found her." The mayor took Eve's hand in his. "A horrible shock, I'm sure. Is there anything I could do for you?"

"No, thank you, Mayor Logan." She pulled her hand free. "We're just stopping by to see the sheriff, then I'm going to pick up Joey and head home."

"Right. Of course. You must be exhausted."

"Let's go, Eve." Mac curved his arm around her waist and turned her toward the door to the jailhouse.

"Hey, I could pick up Joey and bring him back here if it'll save time," Mayor Logan said.

"No, thank you." Eve forced a smile she was sure looked more like a grimace. "We'll only be a few more minutes and I'm not sure he'll go to anyone else."

"He'll be fine." The mayor waved aside her protest. "He's out at the Taylors' house, isn't he?"

"Yes, but—"

"Now, Eve. I insist. You look ready to fall over and you know how I feel responsible for the welfare of the people of Spirit Canyon. Let me do this one thing for you."

"She said no," Mac growled.

Eve laid a hand on Mac's chest. "No, thank you, Mayor Logan. Mac and I will pick him up after we talk to the sheriff."

Mac covered her hand with his, but kept his

gaze on the mayor. "We could go get him before we talk to the sheriff."

"No, we need to take care of business first." She turned to Clint Logan and smiled. "Thank you. I really appreciate your offer."

"As you wish." Mayor Logan smiled and clapped his hands together. "I'll see you two later." He turned and climbed into his Lexus, waving as he backed into the street and headed out of town.

Long after Logan's car disappeared, Mac still stared at the road. "I don't know why, but I just don't trust that man."

Anxious to see Joey, Eve tugged Mac toward the jailhouse. "Come on. Let's get this over with. I want to see my son."

Sheriff Hodges sat at his computer, a frown pressing his brows downward.

"Heard anything from the investigators?" Mac asked.

The older man glanced up as if he didn't realize someone had entered his tiny office. "Oh, hi. Take a seat."

He punched a few more keys and sat back, staring across to the printer on a shelf beyond the desk.

"Thanks for waiting. And yes, I've heard something interesting from the investigative team."

Eve leaned forward, anxious for any clue as to who or what the killer might be. Until it was caught, she didn't feel safe in Spirit Canyon.

"Although the attack appeared to be by an animal, they found human as well as animal footprints in the damp earth nearby."

Mac frowned. "Couldn't the human prints have been one of the people in the search party?"

The sheriff stared across at Mac. "Only if they were barefoot."

Eve frowned. "That's odd."

"And they recovered hairs from beneath Cynthia's fingernails. And those don't appear to be human."

"I don't understand."

"Neither do we. But they've taken the evidence off to the crime lab in Austin. They're expediting the tests so they can get a better idea what we're up against before—" The sheriff glanced at Eve and shut up.

Eve shivered. "Before it happens again." Just the thought of another attack made her energy level plummet. How long had she gone without sleep?

"With Art, we didn't have even one footprint, man or beast. Because Cynthia's death occurred after the storm, we've had more luck with footprints. My only guess is that a person is using his dog to attack people."

"Don't forget the animals who've been killed in a similar fashion," Mac reminded him.

"After Art's death, I requested a query on the crime database to see if we could find a match. We could have a serial killer on our hands. Only, I wasn't sure whether or not they'd have animal attacks in the violent crime database. The only thing even remotely related was something that happened five years ago in a small community outside of Laredo, down along the border." The sheriff tapped a few keys on the computer. "I found the incident. In fact, I was reviewing the electronic archives of the Laredo newspaper for more information. Should have a hit now."

Eve moved to stand behind the sheriff's chair, while Mac leaned over the desk. All three stared at the terminal.

"Seems a woman was mauled to death by a wild animal a little over five years ago. There." Sheriff Hodges clicked on a line and an article appeared, complete with a picture of an older woman, perhaps in her early fifties. Her black hair was heavily streaked with silver. Eve couldn't tell much about the color of her eyes in the black and white photo, only that they were startlingly pale. Probably blue. For an older woman, she was beautiful, in a haunted, hollow-eyed way.

And strangely familiar.

"Why do I feel I've seen this woman before?" Eve asked. "And yet, I'm positive I've never met her."

"I know what you mean." Sheriff Hodges scratched his day-old beard.

Mac stared at the woman in silence, a frown twisting across his brow. Finally he shook his head. "No, I can't put my finger on her. But, like you two said, I feel like I know her."

Eve leaned close to read the newspaper headline. "Local Woman Ravaged by Wolf." She started to read the article. "Joan McGowan. The name doesn't mean anything to me. But this was down around Laredo? For some reason, Laredo is ringing a bell in my head. Someone mentioned it just the other day." That someone was on the edge of her consciousness, but not surfacing. "And this happened five years ago, you say?"

Mac stared at her. "You think you have something?"

"I don't know." Goose bumps rose on her arm. "It's as if this could be really important. But then again, it could be nothing."

"Well, any lead is better than no lead." The radio on the sheriff's shoulder squawked. "Hold on just a minute."

"Sheriff, Toby Rice left his house twenty minutes ago on his four-wheeler. The ATV was headed south across the hills."

"Roger, Bill, come on back to the office." The sheriff rose from his chair. "Before Toby got away last night, he confessed to leaving the dead lamb and the live rattlesnake at Eve's place. Said he was pissed off at her for trying to turn Cynthia against him."

"You think he's the one with the footprint?" Mac asked.

"I don't know. Gotta catch him to get a mold of his foot."

Eve's gaze fell on the computer screen and the face of a woman she didn't know blurred and then came into sharp focus. That something that had hovered on the edge of her brain solidified and hit her square in the chest. The woman in the picture had eyes just like the mayor. The shape of the face, the dark hair laced with gray. She had to be related to Clint Logan.

Chills slithered down her back. "Mac, I recognize this face."

He frowned. "I thought you said you didn't know her."

"I don't." Eve stared into Mac's eyes. "But she looks just like Clint Logan."

"You know, now that you mention it, she does." Sheriff Hodges stared hard at the screen.

"Mayor Logan told me he was from Laredo when he first introduced himself." Eve squeezed her eyes shut trying to remember every detail of that conversation. "He said he arrived in Spirit Canyon five years ago. The timing's right. He could have killed that woman." Panic gripped her like a steel clamp. "Mac, Logan wanted to pick Joey up. If he's the killer, why would he want Joey?"

Mac's frown deepened. "We don't know that he was the woman's killer. It could all be a coincidence."

"Mac, I'd like to get Joey and go home, if you don't mind," Eve said. She wanted her son in her arms and four familiar walls around her. Maybe she'd ask Mac to stay with her. With two potential killers, there could only be trouble in store for Spirit Canyon and Eve didn't feel like being alone.

"You got it. Let's go get Joey." Mac turned toward the door just as the phone on the sheriff's desk rang.

"Sheriff Hodges."

Eve paused, shamelessly eavesdropping for any information about the killer.

As the sheriff listened, he tensed and stared across at Eve. "We'll be there in less than five minutes. Keep calm, Laura. He may just be a few short feet away in the brush."

Laura? Eve's heart jerked to a halt in her chest. "Oh God, something's happened to Joey!" Suddenly she couldn't breathe and she clutched at the desk to keep from falling.

Mac's arm slipped around her and he pulled her against him.

"Mac, he's got Joey. I can feel it." Eve barely breathed; she was only able to take rapid, shallow breaths into her constricted lungs.

Mac turned her in his arms and stared down at her. "Who's got Joey?"

She fought for breath before replying, "The killer."

"Sheriff, we'll be out at the Taylors'." Mac hustled her outside and into his truck, and then climbed in.

Sitting in shocked silence, memories of Joey flashing through her mind, Eve couldn't form a coherent thought. "Oh dear God, I can't lose Joey."

With a vicious jerk, Mac slammed the shift

in Reverse, spinning the truck onto the highway. "No-body's losing anyone. Not on my watch."

"Mac!" Sheriff Hodges ran out the door of his office waving frantically.

Switching from gas to brakes, Mac slammed his foot to the floor, jerking the truck to a halt.

Eve was flung against the safety belt, and what little breath she managed to get past her throat was temporary knocked from her lungs.

The sheriff, his face pale beneath the ruddy tan, leaned both hands against the driver's window and hauled in a deep breath. "I know that woman in the picture, too, Mac."

He shoved a faded photo of three people in Mac's face. "That's me with Frank and Jenny McGuire thirty years ago, Mac." He paused and gulped another lungful of air. "The murdered woman looks just like her. I'd swear she's an older version of Jenny McGuire—your mother."

Mac sat in stunned silence, his truck idling in the middle of the street, his mind idling in a fog as he clutched the dog-eared photograph. He'd seen a copy of this photograph in his father's belongings.

"There must be some mistake." To Mac, Eve's voice sounded as if she was in a tunnel. "Mac doesn't look anything like her."

"Mac looks like his father," the sheriff said. "He never looked like Jenny, except for the eyes."

Eve leaned over Mac's arm to stare at the photo. "Dear God, Clint looks just like your mother."

Eve and Sheriff Hodges's conversation whirled around him and finally congealed. "No matter who that woman was, Joey's missing."

"You think Logan's got him?" The sheriff straightened a frown settling between his brows. "If he's in any way related to Jenny's death…"

"He wanted to pick up Joey." Eve pressed a hand to her mouth, tears welling in her eyes. "We have to find him. Now!"

"Let's go." Mac shifted into Drive.

"Call me with whatever you find. In the meantime, I'll put an APB out for the mayor. And, Mac, I'm sorry."

"It's not your fault." Mac floored the accelerator. As much as the news of his mother hurt, he was more concerned about the little boy he'd grown to love.

During the trip out to the Taylors' they didn't see a single sign of Mayor Logan's Lexus or of Joey.

The sun had sunk to the horizon, melting into the hills and painting the clouds with fire.

The Taylors met them in the driveway. Laura

carried Katie on her hip, her face strained and streaked with dried tears. "I'm so sorry, Eve. One moment the two children were playing, the next, Katie came in asking where Joey was."

Eve hugged Laura briefly, tears slipping silently down her cheeks. Then she straightened and wiped her eyes. "Where did you last see him?"

Laura's lips pressed together as she fought to stem her own tears.

Tom stepped forward. "The kids were playing out back by the swing set."

A cell phone rang several times before Mac realized it was coming from the truck. "We better answer that. If someone took Joey, it might be him."

Eve raced to the truck and snatched Mac's phone from the seat. But she was too late. The voice mail had picked up. She shoved the device at Mac. "See if he left a message."

Mac entered the code for voice mail and his password and waited. "You have one new message. To listen—"

He punched the option to listen and pressed the phone to his ear.

"If you want to see Joey alive, come to the ring of fire." Mac gripped the little device so hard he was afraid it would crack. He knew that smooth tone. Logan. "If you bring the police or anyone else, I'll kill the boy."

Chapter Sixteen

"When we get there, I want you to stay down on the floorboard out of sight." Mac said, his voice hard, unbending.

"No way." Eve stared straight ahead. "That's my son. I'm going with you."

"Eve, be reasonable. I need you to stay put and wait for the sheriff. Why don't you call him now? I have a direct line to his cell on speed dial number two."

She snatched the cell phone from the seat and punched in the number two. When Sheriff Hodges answered, she struggled to stay calm and relay the news. "Logan's taking Joey out to the ring of fire."

"Out by the hog kill?" the sheriff asked.

"Yes. We're headed there now."

"Give me the phone." Mac held out his hand. "Logan said he'd kill the boy if I called in the police. I don't know what to tell you, but keep it quiet. We're not going to wait for you. We can't."

Temporary relief flooded Eve. Mac wasn't going to insist she stay behind. Not that it would have meant a difference. Wild horses couldn't keep her away from her son. Then the first part of what Mac had said sank in.

He closed the phone and handed it back to Eve.

Eve glared at him. "You didn't tell me that last part. You didn't tell me Logan was going to kill Joey."

"And what would you have done differently, had you known?" He shot a glance at her, then turned his attention back to the road, pressing harder on the accelerator.

"I wouldn't have called the sheriff." She waved her hand in the air. "My son could be killed because of this."

"We need the backup, Eve. Maybe if I'd had backup in Iraq, my troops wouldn't have died."

"Mac, this isn't about your troops. This is about my son. I won't let anything happen to him." Eve grabbed for the phone. "I'm calling the sheriff and telling him to back off. We don't need his help."

Mac covered her hand over the cell phone. "Trust me, Eve. I love that little boy and don't want anything to happen to him, any more than you do. But we need the sheriff involved. What if we're up against the entire cult?"

Tears sprang to her eyes. "I can't lose Joey. I can't."

"We're not going to. He's tough and you are, too." He squeezed her hand, cell phone and all. "That's why I fell in love with you."

Eve stared at him, her eyes wide, haunted, then her fingers slipped from beneath his and she sat quietly in her corner of the truck cab.

Had he gone too far telling her he loved her? They hadn't known each other very long and he knew how she felt about stepfathers. "Forget I just said that, and don't worry, I won't get in the way of your raising Joey. Because you *will* raise that little boy and we *will* get him back safe and sound."

His hands clenched on the steering wheel. Logan better not hurt one hair on that kid's head or he'd have hell to pay.

They turned off the road, bumped and slid along the trail leading down toward the river on Frantzen's ranch. Other vehicles had made the trek before them, the recent rains having made the hint of a road a mucky, rutted nightmare.

By the time they reached the open field, night had cloaked the hills in darkness. Clouds scudded across the star-filled sky and a full moon rose in the east, a sinister glow circling the pale orange orb.

On a night like this, anything could happen. Dread filled Mac's chest, but he tamped it down. He had a kid to find and a killer to deal with. And there was the little matter of his mother he wanted clarified.

EVE SCANNED the field for any sign of Logan or Joey. "Are we in the wrong place?"

"No, we walk from here." Mac climbed down and circled the truck to stand beside Eve. He pulled her into his arms and pressed a kiss to her mouth. "Let's go get Joey." He clicked his tongue and Molly leaped from the bed of the truck and followed along behind them.

Eve's lips tingled with the lingering sensation of Mac's kiss. As she tramped through the damp, knee-high spear grass, she alternated between the enigma who was Mac and the fear of losing her son. Thinking about Mac and what he'd told her helped her focus and kept her from hyperventilating over the mortal danger looming over Joey.

Had she been wrong to push away from this man? Ever since she'd met him, he'd been a positive influence in her and Joey's life. Could a man change his entire character just because they got married? Eve shook her head. Not Mac. He was solid, through and through. And he'd said he loved her. Eve hugged his words to herself, letting them ward off the rising panic.

They approached a stand of scrub cedar and stunted red oaks. Through the branches Eve could see the glow of a fire. The fire from her nightmare.

She stumbled, pitching into Mac's back. To right herself, she grabbed on to the back of his belt.

"You okay?" he whispered, his arm circling her waist until she stood steady beside him.

"Just clumsy." She pushed aside a branch and stared into the clearing on the other side, her heart lodged firmly in her throat, a full-scale panic attack threatening to engulf her. The scene was exactly like her dream. "Do you see Joey?"

"Not yet."

The fiery ring sent a glow skyward, the pungent scent of mesquite and burning oak filling the air. Then a man in a black hooded cape stepped into the circle carrying her son.

Eve gasped. It was just like in her dream, except the sacrificial lamb was Joey.

Simultaneously, she and Mac pushed through the cedar break.

"Let him go!" Eve cried, racing across the field toward her son.

Mac caught her and stopped her short of the circle of cloaked men. "Logan, let the boy go."

When Joey saw them through the flames, he reached out his little arms and screamed, "Mac!"

Eve's heart caught in her chest. That was the first time he'd uttered a word since his father died. And now, in a sick twist of fate, her son was in an equally perilous situation that could mean his own death.

But Eve couldn't think that way. Her son would live, even if she had to give her own life to save his.

Mac spoke again. "He's not the one you're after, Logan."

"No?" The caped figure shoved the hood from his head, revealing who Eve already knew he was. Clint Logan. "And how would you figure that?"

"You want me."

"Well, you're only half-right about that, brother." This last word he spat like venom. "I'm saving you for last." He waved his free hand toward the wall of caped figures.

They moved in and surrounded Mac and Eve.

"Jack, Hank," Mac said, looking at the men, "I've known you all my life. Don't make me hurt you."

The two men jerked to a halt.

"What do you know about hurting people?" Jack Adams asked. He pushed back his hood and stood in the glow of the flames, an angry scowl giving him a sinister look in the limited light. "It's ranchers like you that put the rest of us out of business."

"Your own financial decisions and lousy weather did that, not anyone else." Mac crouched in a ready stance beside Eve. "Don't make it any worse on yourself. My bet is Logan killed Art and Cynthia. Don't let him drag you down, too."

Hank Bleumfeld pushed his hood back and glared at Mac. "Don't listen to him. He's one of the enemy. He would own every ranch around here if you let him get away with it."

"I didn't sign on to kill anyone," Jack shot back at Hank. He turned back to Mac. "Logan's the one that told me I had to run you and Dan off the road."

Mac's lips thinned into a straight line. "You almost got Dan killed."

"Logan said he'd kill us if we went against him," Jack said in a low voice.

Logan roared. "Damn right I will. You stand as my brothers, or you die."

Jack turned on Logan. "Art was one of us, but you killed him."

"He dared to disagree with the pack."

"He disagreed with you! And you killed him," Hank said. "We ain't never killed no people."

"You're either with me or against me." Logan held Joey high above his head.

The boy screamed and struggled against the hands holding him around the middle.

Eve watched in horror. She was desperate to go to her child, but afraid Logan would hurt him if she tried to break through his line of henchmen.

"He's manipulating you, Hank. Don't fall victim to him," Mac continued.

"That monster killed Cynthia. He needs to die!" Toby appeared out of the darkness in jeans and a T-shirt. Gone was his cocky attitude. In its place was a hollow-eyed boy, barely out of his teens. "You killed her!" When Toby would have charged into the ring of fire, Mac stepped forward and caught him by the arm.

"Don't. He might hurt the boy," Mac said.

"But he killed my Cynthia." Toby dropped to his knees and sobbed into his hands.

"Now that my audience is complete, shall I sacrifice the boy to the Cult of the Wolf?"

Eve lurched forward. "No!"

"Mommy?" Joey squirmed to get down. "Mommy!"

Mac's chest tightened at the boy's fearful

cries, and his fists clenched at his sides. Yet he held his anger in check. He couldn't let Logan hurt Joey or Eve. He had to stay a mental step ahead of the other man. He had to keep Clint talking until he could figure out how to handle the situation. "Logan, why did you call me brother? I'm not a member of the cult."

"Because that's what we are. Half brothers, to be exact. We shared the same mother." Logan lowered the boy, clamping him to his waist with an arm around the child's belly.

Mac shook his head. "You're crazy. I was an only child."

"That's what *Mom* wanted you to think. I'm twenty-nine years old and you're what, thirty-four? When did she abandon you, Mac? You do the math."

"Liar." Mac's hands rose, ready to charge through the line of men and smash Clint's face. "My mother would never have cheated on my father."

"Oh, everyone is under the impression our mother was attacked by a wolf. They were right, in a way. The legends call us werewolves. Did you know Art Nantan was of Apache descent?"

"What's that got to do with my mother? And what is this crap about werewolves?"

"I bet you didn't know he wanted your

mother, did you? He wanted her so badly back then, he used an old Indian ritual to unleash the spirit of the wolf. That would be my father. The creature that raped your mother." Logan laughed. "He was supposed to kill your father, which he ultimately did by default, when your mother disappeared."

Mac's mind chewed on Clint's words. Thirty years ago, to this day, his mother had been attacked. Could Clint be telling the truth?

"She left you when she found out she was pregnant with me." Clint slapped his free hand against his chest. "Me!" The younger man's face morphed, his nose lengthening into a snout, his teeth enlarging to razor-sharp fangs. "She wanted to spare her family the pain of learning she'd been impregnated by a monster. Because, as you see, my father and I are not quite human and not quite wolf."

"Joey! Close your eyes. Close them tight!" Eve yelled.

Mac's mind reeled. Why didn't his mother tell his father? As soon as the thought occurred, he remembered what had really happened. Mac's father hadn't let his mother talk about the experience. Each time his mother tried to talk about it, his father had interrupted, telling her that it didn't matter, that everything would be all right. Instead of protecting her, Frank Mc-Guire's act of love had driven his wife into hiding.

"She always said we had the same eyes," Logan continued. "Her beloved Mac. She never got over you and your father. But she stayed with me, hoping I wouldn't turn out to be like my father. And I hid it as long as I could."

Clint's eyebrows grew shaggier and he emitted a snarling growl. "She always loved you best, talking about how kind and helpful you were as a boy. When she learned about your father's death, she packed her bag. She was going to leave me to go back to you."

Mac stood in stunned silence, Clint's entire tale too incredible. As the creature transformed before his eyes, Mac had no choice but to believe. "You killed my mother, didn't you?"

"I wouldn't let her go. I threatened to kill you if she went back." Logan half laughed, half growled. "When I was sixteen, she tried to kill me." Clint flung his head back. "My own mother tried to kill me! Just because I was different." He howled, a long, anguished sound. Hairs erupted from his skin, filling in bare space with silver bristles.

Eve stirred, her face a picture in anguish. "Joey, keep your eyes closed, honey. Everything will be okay."

"Mommy." The little boy whimpered. "I want my mommy."

"Let my son go," Eve pleaded. "You can take me instead. I'll take his place."

"No!" Mac's hand shot out, clamping on her arm. "Don't, Eve." He knew if he let her go, he might never see her again. Mac had lost almost everyone he'd ever cared about. He couldn't lose Eve and Joey, too. She and the little boy would be gone, just like his mother, his father and his troops.

"I have to do this, Mac." She lea .ed up and kissed his lips, then shook loose of his grip and moved toward Clint. "Let Joey go and you can have me."

"How touching." Clint sneere.l, exposing long, razor-sharp teeth. "That's a tempting proposition. Let her through." The wall of caped figures parted.

When Eve stood before him, the ring of fire was the only thing standing between them. Clint reached out and jerked her into the circle, at the same time dropping Joey outside the fire.

When Eve reached for Joey, Logan back-handed her, knocking her to the dirt, just inches from the flames. She lay there, unmoving.

"No!" Mac's heart thundered in his chest. He

lurched forward, but Joey hit him at the knees. He couldn't move forward without hurting the boy. With a frustrated growl, he hauled Joey into his arms and stared across the fire at Logan.

"She's mine now, brother." Logan's body was now covered with a sheen of slivery fur, his snout elongated to the size of a wolf's. The wolf-man stalked the curve of the ring, stopping to nudge Eve with his toe. With a laugh, he turned his snout to the moon and howled.

The child pressed his face into Mac's chest and whimpered.

"Joey, I need you to be a tough guy and go to Jack." He handed the boy to Jack Adams, his eyes narrowing into slits. "Hurt one hair on that kid's head, and I'll personally rip your limbs off with my bare hands."

Jack took Joey and nodded. "We didn't kill anyone, Mac."

"You've done enough damage. Keep the boy safe." Then he turned to Logan. "Let her go, Logan. You want me."

"That's right. I want you." The creature prowled the circle, his face a mix of man and wolf. "I killed our mother, just like I'll kill you."

"Like you killed Art and Cynthia?"

"Art was a fool playing with more power than he knew what to do with." Clint snorted. "And that stupid blabbing teenager Cynthia needed to be shut up."

A shout sounded next to Mac. Toby Rice lurched to his feet and barreled into the fiery ring, yelling all the way. "You bastard. You murdering bastard. She wasn't stupid. You killed my Cynthia. The only good thing in my life." He charged in like a football lineman. Logan stood his ground and just as Toby neared him, he swept a clawed hand out hitting the young man in the neck. As if Toby weighed no more than a child, he was flung to the side and lay still and bleeding in the dirt.

Behind Logan, Eve stirred.

Mac held his breath. Stay still, he urged her silently. Anger threatened to overwhelm Mac, but he couldn't lose his cool. Eve's life depended on him. Mac had to stop Clint.

"After you're dead, I'll take your woman as my own and breed her like my father did our mother."

"Like hell you will." Mac dove through the ring of fire, hitting Clint in his furry belly.

The wolf-man staggered backward and took a swing at Mac.

But Mac was ready. He dove to the side, springing to his feet. Without a weapon, he didn't stand much of a chance in the fight against this monster that claimed to be his brother.

"Watch out, Mac!" Eve called. "He's strong. Too strong." She pulled herself to her feet and threw a fist-size rock at Clint. "Run, Mac! Save yourself!"

The rock hit Clint in the side of the head. He roared and spun toward his new attacker.

Mac's chest swelled. Eve cared enough about him to sacrifice herself for his safety. Just like a woman. Just like his mother.

The beast leaped at Eve, knocking her to her knees. He opened his long snout and aimed for her throat.

"No!" Mac rushed at Clint. With all the force he could pack behind one hundred and ninety pounds of angry male and steel-toed cowboy boots, he kicked the creature in the ribs.

The wolf-man roared and rolled to the side, then back to his four feet. "I've had enough of you, brother."

Behind Clint, Eve staggered to her feet, and reaching into her pocket, she pulled out the knife he'd given her.

"Good, Logan, because I'm ready to end this little party." Mac forced a cocky smile to curve his lips, determined to keep the creature's attention on himself.

"It will end only with your death!" Clint lunged at Mac's throat, his jagged teeth bared.

Mac grabbed for Clint's neck and held on for all he was worth. The beast knocked him to the rocky ground where Mac struggled to hang on despite the superior strength of the writhing, fur-covered body snapping at his jugular vein. His muscles bulged and his arms shook as he struggled to keep those jagged teeth from claiming his life. He couldn't die. Eve and Joey needed him.

A flash of mottle-colored fur flew across Mac's peripheral vision as Molly leaped into the fray. A quarter the size of Logan, she made up for her limited bulk by ferocity. She bit and tore at the animal's hindquarters, providing enough distraction for Mac to manage the downward pressure Logan was exerting on him.

Then Logan kicked out hard and fast, catching Molly in the side of the head and slinging her to the ground. She lay stunned and still, whimpering a few times before she quieted.

Without the dog biting at his backside, Logan threw all his effort into killing Mac.

Eve moved in holding the knife high.

"Kill him, Eve!" Mac shouted.

She appeared over Clint, the knife's blade locked in place. With both hands, she held the weapon over the wolf's body. "This is for Cynthia," she said, her voice loud and clear. She plunged the knife deep into Clint's back.

The animal threw back his head and roared. The movement weakened Logan's attack but not enough for Mac to break free.

"And this is for Jenny McGuire." Eve lifted the knife and plunged it into him again, her face a determined mask.

Mac shoved with all his strength and tossed Clint to the side. His heart thundering in his chest, he rolled to his feet.

Clint limped a few steps away, snarling, his breathing ragged. "If that's the way you want to play it…" He turned on Eve. "Your woman dies."

Eve moved closer and stood with her feet braced. She lifted the knife again. "Over my dead body."

His lip curling into a snarl, Clint said, "Precisely." The beast crouched.

"No, Eve!" Mac lunged at Logan, but missed him as he sprang toward Eve.

In a flash of fur, the creature was on top of Eve, knocking her knife out of her hands and into the darkness. The beast's powerful jaws opened wide, and razor-sharp teeth sank into Eve's throat.

Adrenaline rushed through Mac's veins as he fell onto Clint. "Die, you bastard!" He hooked an arm around the creature's neck and clamped off the flow of air. Clint didn't move, his teeth were still clenched in Eve's throat.

Eyes wide, her face losing all color, Eve stared up at Mac.

The creature's jaw slackened and he lurched to the side, falling on to his back.

"Holy hell, what's that?" A flashlight shined onto the werewolf from the darkness as Sheriff Hodges rushed forward. Others joined him, all stopping to stare at the animal.

Mac's gaze swept over Eve. He stripped his shirt from his back and pressed it to the jagged wound in her throat, holding it tight enough to stop the bleeding, but not so tight she couldn't breathe. "You're going to be all right, darling." He bent low to press a kiss to her forehead, thanking God the teeth hadn't ripped into her jugular vein. He turned to the sheriff. "Call for a chopper. She needs medical assistance."

The sheriff, his gaze still locked on the creature, shook his head before answering. "The Med-Flight is on its way. They should be here in less than fifteen minutes."

"Mac?" Eve's voice was a hoarse, gravelly whisper. She raised her hand to his cheek.

"Shh, baby." He clutched her fingers and pressed a kiss to the tips. "Don't talk."

"I…need…to…say…"

"Later, sweetheart. You can talk later after the doctor has taken care of your injuries."

"No, now."

Mac smiled down at her stubborn frown and wanted to crush her in his arms. He loved this woman more than life, and he'd almost lost her. Leaning closer, he smoothed the hair from her face. "Okay, baby, shoot."

"I was wrong." Eve stared up into his face, a tear seeping from the corner of her eyes.

With a gentle touch, he caught the tear with the tip of his finger. "Wrong about what?"

"I want you in my life." Eve's body shook with a weak cough.

More men entered the clearing and spoke in shocked murmurs, but Mac heard the words barely spoken above a whisper. His heart beat a rapid tattoo against his ribs as hope rose inside him. "What about Joey? You know I love that kid. But if I'm in his life, I'd be his stepfather."

Eve pressed her hand to his lips. "No, you'd be his father."

In a rocky field in the middle of the Texas hill country, Mac McGuire's chest swelled as he held the hand of the woman he loved. "Eve, will you marry me?"

"Yes." She didn't hesitate, her green eyes gleaming in her pale face. "I love you, Mac, and even more importantly I trust you with my son's happiness."

Mac pressed his cheek to hers, wanting to pull her into his arms but afraid of hurting her. He chuckled. This was the first time he'd felt really happy since his mother had left. "When we get you out of here and all fixed up, I'll make a more appropriate proposal. One more fitting the woman I love."

With her eyes drifting shut, Eve smiled. "I liked it just the way it was."

"Look! He's changing!" The sheriff's voice called out above the murmuring crowd of men.

Mac tore his gaze from Eve long enough to witness the werewolf's transformation back into the brother he never knew.

"Makes you wonder if there are any more out there like him," Sheriff Hodges said in an awed whisper.

"I hope not," Mac said. "Look at the lives just this one destroyed."

"Mommy?" Joey struggled in Jack's arms until the man let him down. "Mommy, don't go away."

"I'm not, honey. I'll be all right. You'll see." Her voice was weak, but her grip in Mac's hand was strong. She was a fighter and he loved her all the more for it.

"She'll be all right, little man. We'll all be all right together." Mac pulled the boy into his spare arm and hugged him.

Molly nudged her way into the little group gathered around Eve and licked Joey's face.

"Molly's a good dog." Joey hugged the dog's neck and received another lick for his effort.

"Yes, Molly's a good dog." Mac stared down at what was to be his new family and smiled.

"Mac?" Eve said, her eyelashes drifting down to brush against her cheeks.

"Yes, darling?"

"Your mother loved you."

"I know that now." Moisture threatened to fill his eyes. All these years he'd hated what his mother had done to his family. He wished he could tell her how sorry he was. Tell her he loved her for her sacrifice.

Eve opened her eyes again. "Thank you for saving my life."

His lips pressed together and he adjusted his shirt more snugly against the wound at her throat. "I almost cost you your life."

"But I'm not going to die." Her eyes opened and she smiled up at him and Joey.

"Not if I can help it."

"Mac?" Eve squeezed his hand.

"Yes, baby?" He smoothed the hair from her forehead.

Her eyelids sank downward again. "Do you

think there are any more of those creatures out there?"

Could the wolf spirit Art Nantan unleashed have created more of his kind in the Texas hill country? More than Mac's half brother, Clint? Mac stared out across the moonlit landscape, the hairs on the back of his neck rising to stand at attention. "Let's hope not, baby. Let's hope not."

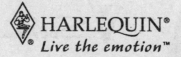

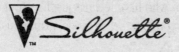

HARLEQUIN®
Presents

The world's bestselling romance series...
The series that brings you your favorite authors,
month after month:

Helen Bianchin...Emma Darcy
Lynne Graham...Penny Jordan
Miranda Lee...Sandra Marton
Anne Mather...Carole Mortimer
Susan Napier...Michelle Reid

and many more uniquely talented authors!

Wealthy, powerful, gorgeous men...
Women who have feelings just like your own...
The stories you love, set in exotic, glamorous locations...

HARLEQUIN®
Presents

Seduction and Passion Guaranteed!

HPDIR104

Harlequin Historicals®
Historical Romantic Adventure!

From rugged lawmen and valiant knights to defiant heiresses and spirited frontierswomen, Harlequin Historicals will capture your imagination with their dramatic scope, passion and adventure.

Harlequin Historicals . . . they're too good to miss!

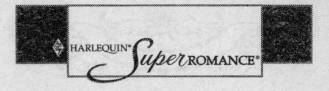
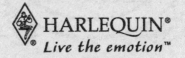

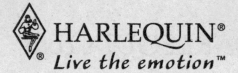

HARLEQUIN®
Live the emotion™

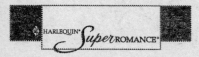